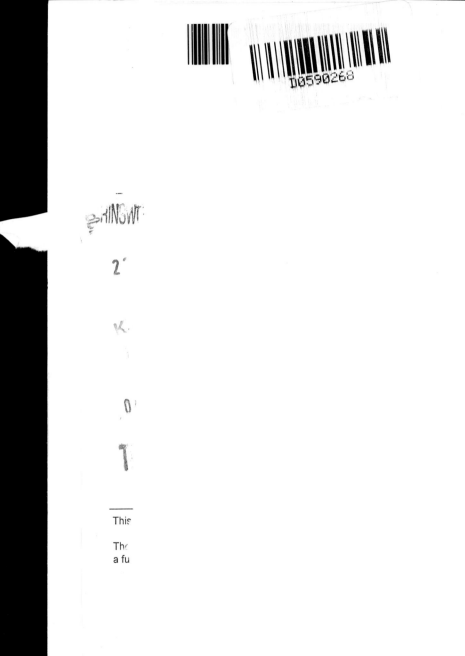

BRINSW

2

K.

0

T

This

The
a fu

The Magnificent Mendozas

When the Mexican circus ships out of the gringo town of Conejos Blancos, Hart and his ruthless desperadoes are quick off the mark to take over the town, and the adjacent silver mine.

With the sheriff slaughtered, and many of the citizens held hostage, two local boys escape, and recruit seven Mexican circus performers to help penetrate the cordon of sentries and free the townspeople. Only the 'Magnificent Mendozas' – a family of weapons experts, escapologists and gymnasts – stand a chance against the Hart gang, but there will be betrayal, bravery and plenty of action, on both sides of the divide before the day is through.

The Magnificent Mendozas

Ross Morton

A Black Horse Western

ROBERT HALE · LONDON

© Ross Morton 2014
First published in Great Britain 2014

ISBN 978-0-7198-1322-1

Robert Hale Limited
Clerkenwell House
Clerkenwell Green
London EC1R 0HT

www.halebooks.com

Typeset by
Derek Doyle & Associates, Shaw Heath
Printed and bound in Great Britain by
CPI Antony Rowe, Chippenham and Eastbourne

To Jennifer, my wife and best friend, and Hannah, Harry and Darius

PROLOGUE

TIMING WAS EVERYTHING

Friday

Rope restraints prevented Josefa Mendoza from moving her svelte body out of harm's way. Wrists and ankles tethered, she felt her insides churn in fearful anticipation. Her cinnamon skin was beaded with sweat.

Abruptly, an enormous knife blade thudded into the wood to the left of her ear and tiny grains of sawdust powdered her bare shoulder. The sound was deafening as it hit.

But she was used to this. Not so, the Conejos Blancos audience, who collectively lapsed into fearful silence. The band's drummer played up the suspense, beating a tense rataplan on the skins.

Mateo narrowed his dark velvet eyes. Josefa loved those eyes, trusted them implicitly. His second Bowie knife imbedded itself in the board to the right of her head. A tad closer, she estimated, and it would have sheared off a swatch of her long raven-black hair.

The crowd gasped as, in quick succession, Mateo let fly six

more knives; they sank into the wood under her armpits, on either side of her waist, between her spread-eagled legs and, finally, impaled her feathered headdress above her scalp. That was close, too – she was sure she felt the blade tug at her hair.

Spontaneous applause erupted in the big tent as Mateo took his bow.

Then he strode over, smiling, idly stroking his Cadiz beard. He deftly cut her bonds with one of the thrown knives – a nice touch, just to prove they really were sharp.

Garbed in her green sequined leotard and Aztec princess regalia, Josefa bowed. She was pleased to note she got the biggest cheer from the audience, much to her husband's amusement. As he often said, 'A pretty girl wins hearts over skill any day!'

Judging by the flushed, freckled cheeks of a young boy watching from the sidelines, his blue eyes like saucers, she'd already won at least one heart today. Straw-coloured hair unkempt, his dungarees patched, the boy was about fourteen, she guessed. She was willing to bet that he was ripe for running away with the circus. But he didn't have the courage to make the move.

Just to the right of the boy, she noticed José, Mateo's younger brother, his eyes still lustful for her. He shouldn't be eyeing her up; he should be getting ready for his trick-riding act. *Caramba!* He was becoming a pest. He wanted her just because he was 'more her age', as he said. 'Leave that old man and ride into the sunset with me!' he implored her. True, he was taller than Mateo, and there was a considerable age difference between them; he was fifteen years younger than his brother and it showed in his demeanour, though she didn't dare tell him that. He had quite a rage in him, José; he was in many ways like his friend Antonio with his honeyed words, but at least Antonio respected women. She wasn't too sure about

José. She didn't trust him; every aspect of him made her shudder.

The farmer visibly shuddered as he sat down. Lee Grant prided himself on having that effect on some men. The scar from temple to chin probably intimidated them, too. The town of Mogote was small, with a sizeable farming community who thrived on the rich soil; many of them seemed to enjoy gambling as a break from the hard graft and monotony of their chosen lifestyle, which suited Grant just fine.

The few bystanders gathered around the table watched intently. The saloon murmuring had quelled into a hushed noise, like a whisper. There was tension in the air. Maybe it had to do with the heap of greenbacks piled in the centre of the table.

'Are you going to show me your cards or not?' Grant demanded.

'I – I reckon I'll fold . . .' the farmer said and lowered his cards face down. 'I'm cleaned out.'

'That suits me fine.' Grant turned to the only other remaining opponent. He was dressed like a dandy, he reckoned. Maybe a cardsharp.

'Sir, Mr Grant,' said a man to the right.

Grant pressed his cards to his chest and turned in his chair.

The man from the telegraph office hovered, wafting a yellow sheet of paper. 'I got this urgent message, sir. Just like you said, I came as soon as I got it.'

'Thanks.' Grant took the message and passed the telegrapher a dollar.

'Much obliged. Will there be a reply, Mr Grant?'

'Probably.' He eyed the dandy, who seemed quite impatient now. 'I'll just win this hand of cards then I'll be right over.'

'Right, sir. I'll be waiting.' The telegrapher hurried out of the saloon.

'Who said you'd win?' the dandy growled.

'My cards say it, unless you've been holding out on me.'

'What are you implying, Grant?'

He shrugged. 'You know, well enough.'

The dandy moved fast, left hand drawing a derringer from his vest pocket.

Grant was fast, too. His Bowie knife left its sheath inside his vest, flew across the table and sank into the dandy's chest before the derringer could be fired.

The bystanders backed off, some whispering, 'My God, did you see that?'

The dandy stared at the hilt protruding from his chest. His cards tumbled from his fingers – the ace, king and queen of hearts plus the ace of spades and the ace of clubs.

Still remaining seated, Grant placed his cards face up on the table. 'Well, look at that – I've got three aces and two kings. . . .'

The revelation that either Grant or the dandy had cheated caused more of a stir than the fatal knife, it seemed. Men clustered and stared at the cards.

Grant opened the message sheet. It was brief: *Meet me at Mesita with your men. Hart.*

He nodded, pleased. It wouldn't take him long to alert Chip, Vince and Bernie. He stood and leaned over the table, gathered up the bills, saying, 'I'd better take my winnings.'

'Wha— what about him?' someone asked, pointing at the dandy, who was still alive, breathing heavily.

'You're right, I'm being forgetful,' Grant smiled. 'Get him an undertaker.' He tossed twenty dollars on the table. 'That should cover it.' Then he withdrew the knife, wiped it on the dandy's jacket and slid it into its sheath.

Finally, the dandy fell forward, his face making a mess of the table's surface as it hit.

*

10

Diego Vallejo, the circus owner, beamed as the brass band blared, trumpeting the bravery of Josefa. Surely, he had plenty of good acts – and animals – but the Mendoza troupe always drew the biggest crowds.

Next to perform was the olive-skinned 18-year-old Arcadia Mendoza. Wearing a white leotard that showed off her hourglass figure, she entered the ring on stilts, followed by two clowns on even taller stilts, though theirs were concealed by very long striped trousers. She crossed the sawdust arena and abruptly jumped off the stilts, her long nut-brown ponytail flicking, then somersaulted and landed on a low tightrope, where she wavered and then balanced. Amid rapturous applause, she then leaped into the air and this time was caught by Juan Suarez as he swung down on a trapeze.

Diego smiled. Arcadia seemed fearless, her dark brown slanted eyes showing no concern. Nobody watching would know that Arcadia's father, Rafael, fell to his death a mere two years ago, in Tijuana.

Juan Suarez was a tough *hombre*, with muscles like iron, a worthy replacement for her father. Their trapeze act was perfect. Gradually, the pair swung from trapeze to trapeze, going higher and higher into the peak of the big top, where hung three brass bells. He scanned the crowd. Every one of the audience craned their neck, watching fearfully. Daring and fear drew the crowds. And of course timing was everything in a performance.

Now, Arcadia walked a tightrope while carrying a bow and several arrows. Diego's mouth went dry. There was no safety net. Yet this was her toughest act so far. In quick succession, she fired three arrows at the bells – and they clanged resoundingly. Then, from the opposite end of the tightrope, Juan fired an arrow at her – people gasped, and in the same instant she caught the arrow between her palms. They cheered, amazed, while she still swayed ever so slightly on the tightrope.

Finally, she lit a taper on the end of her last arrow, and then shot it towards the ceiling. Before it could pierce the canvas, it exploded and sprayed into thousands of scintillating lights.

'Fireworks!'

Juan let off more fireworks that cascaded down into the circus ring.

The audience went wild. Some thought it was like the Fourth of July.

'Fireworks should happen any time soon,' Mack Calhoun said as he stood nonchalantly on the saloon veranda, leaning his big frame against the upright post, waiting.

Taking him at his word, the people, who moments earlier had frequented Hicktown's main street, now deserted it. A few brave souls peered through windows or over the batwings of the saloons.

He didn't have long to wait.

Sheriff Roper exited the telegraph office in a hurry, one hand grasping a yellow sheet. And then he paused, eyeing Calhoun.

'You've outstayed your welcome in my town, Calhoun,' the sheriff said. 'I've just got word from the marshal – you're wanted for murder. . . .'

Calhoun's grey eyes narrowed and he drew his pistol and fanned the hammer. All six shots punched into the sheriff's chest. 'That's true – so I may as well be hanged for yours as well as all the others.'

He walked over to the dead lawman, leaned down and tugged not one but two telegram sheets from the deathly clasp.

He pushed the brim of his hat up with the snout of his smoking pistol. 'Well, Sheriff, I'm ashamed of you – reading another man's telegram!' The first told Sheriff Roper of

Calhoun's nefarious past and advised extreme caution. The marshal who sent the telegram suggested Roper wait until he could be reinforced. 'Impetuous fool,' Calhoun mused. Then he read the second message, which was addressed to him: *Meet me with your men at Mesita. Hart.*

Calhoun rose and holstered his gun. Three swarthy men stepped out of the shadows, leading four horses, and joined him.

As he mounted up, Calhoun studied the doors and windows. 'This town's got the right name, boys. It's full of hicks with no guts. We've stayed too long – now we ride to Mesita!'

'What for, Boss?'

'An old friend who promised a while back he'd send for me when the big score was due. I reckon now is the time.'

'Score?' asked another.

Calhoun chuckled. 'We're going to get rich, boys. Filthy rich!'

CHAPTER 1

THE MEXICAN PROCESS

Besides Juan Suarez, Diego mused, the only other troupe member not belonging to the Mendoza family was Antonio Rivera. Originally, he'd been hired by Mateo to replace Arcadia's father but they soon learned he brought in more interest from the crowds as a sharpshooter. He needed watching; Antonio was a ladies' man, with his tanned, toned body, raven-black hair cut short, deep brown eyes and pencil-thin moustache.

Now, José Mendoza entered the ring standing straddle-legged on the backs of two white horses, holding the reins with one hand, waving a rifle with the other. He was sinewy and tanned. Behind him the horses pulled a four-wheeled cart.

In the bed of the cart was a large wooden box. Diego stroked his goatee, ruminating. The troupe's acts seemed to blend from one to the next, smoothly. The wooden box would shortly become part of Ramón Mendoza's escapologist trickery.

Although Conejos Blancos was a small town, it seemed to

welcome the circus with open arms – and open wallets. People from all around flocked to watch; farmers, ranchers – their wagons lined up in every street. It was a prosperous place, Diego reflected, in part thanks to the silver mine situated at the northwest corner of the town, which spread down the small mountainside and seemed to end at a compound at the mountain's base.

At different levels of the mountainside were buildings, and some of these had chimneys that belched noxious fumes. Others made strange grinding noises.

Halfway up the mountainside was a gaping hole, bored into the rock. From here several sets of pulleys worked lengths of cable down to the main mine entrance. Swinging at the bottom of these cables were large metal buckets, big enough to hold two men – or lots of ore. Clearly, ore was transported up the mountain to the processing buildings.

Spread on the hardpan next to the cable winch mechanism was a pile of silver, presumably dumped from one of these buckets.

The hardpan area in front of the main mine entrance was surrounded by a wood stockade, with a lookout tower at either end. The road from the mine ran alongside the creek, past the town hall that was at the head of Main Street, continued along the edge of the creek, crossed a bridge and opened up into the northern road that led to Colorado Springs and ultimately Denver. Rabbit Creek looped south and created the natural limit of the town. To the east of the creek was marshland.

On his first day in the town, following the grand entry parade, Diego had been invited into the mine compound by Simeon Gray, the owner. Dressed in his red and blue serape, bolero jacket, tight pants and high boots, Diego wished to make an impression.

Gray was dressed in a business-like manner, a light grey suit, white shirt and thin black tie. 'From one businessman to another,' he said, arms akimbo in the entrance, 'I'd take it kindly if you'd dissuade any thimble-riggers and chuck-a-luckers from fleecing my men. They've worked damned hard in the mine, I'd hate them to get short-changed by your sideshow johnnies.'

Withdrawing his sombrero and bowing knowingly, Diego smiled. 'I heartily agree, Mr Gray. I have a small but effective contingent of stout fellows armed with cudgels who delight in catching those moths that hover around my candle. I can assure you that there will be no sideshows allowed other than those belonging to me and my circus. And we're bona fide.'

'Very well.' Gray shook his hand, which was a fine feeling, Diego reckoned. Many gringos would barely deign to touch a Mexican, unless it was with a boot. 'Let me show you my mine!'

'I'm honoured, *señor.*'

The complex was a series of two-storey wooden buildings in a horseshoe shape around the three mine entrances in the side of the mountain. The horseshoe was broken by a gap in the building line, with an arch built over it.

Simeon Gray led Diego up the flight of creaking wood stairs to the office situated over the arch. 'It's a neat arrangement,' Gray said, as they reached the balustrade-enclosed balcony, 'so I can watch the coming and going of the ore-laden wagons.'

'Yes.' Diego nodded. 'You have a splendid view from here.'

Gray was effusive. He explained that wagons and stables were on the left arm of the horseshoe, while miners lived in their quarters on the right arm. 'They work two shifts, seven hours each. Of course, it isn't on the scale of the Montezuma find in Summit County, or even Leadville five years back.'

They entered the office, which was quite spacious. It had a window on the left, another directly opposite the only door, behind a big broad desk, and a third on the right. Two walls on the left were lined with shelves crammed with files and papers. A small, bulky cast-iron safe sat to one side of the desk. There were only two chairs, so Gray clearly didn't expect people to sit around in here.

Diego strode over to the window on the right, near the desk and remarked on a two-storey watchtower to the right of the mine entrance.

'This investment needs protection, Señor Vallejo. Silver's mighty valuable,' Gray said, grinning. 'But you don't need me to tell you that!'

Diego smiled. 'We have a fortune teller who would keenly have you cross her hands with silver, Señor Gray!'

At that moment, a young woman entered the office and flew towards Gray.

'Pa!' she exclaimed, her blue gingham skirts flouncing as she ran.

'I've just heard there's a clairvoyant with the circus!' Then, abruptly, she stopped almost in mid-stride, noticing her father had company. 'Oh, I'm sorry, Pa, sir. . . .' She flushed, which added charm to her magnolia pink complexion. Her corn-flower-blue eyes pierced Diego's as she boldly held out her hand. 'Sir, my father is remiss, he hasn't introduced us.'

'Señor Vallejo, this is my headstrong, intemperate daughter Naomi.' The mine owner smiled indulgently at Naomi. 'She's seventeen going on thirty-two!'

'Pa!'

Gently, Diego took her hand and bowed with a slight flourish. 'Miss, I am enchanted. I am Diego Vallejo, the circus owner. I—'

'Can I visit your fortune teller, sir, Señor Vallejo?' She glanced at her father, as if for permission, and he simply shrugged.

Diego nodded. 'It is quite harmless, I assure you both.'

'Wait till I tell Lily!' Then she swerved on her heels and rushed out.

Simeon Gray laughed. 'She keeps me young – or does she make me feel my age?'

Diego nodded. 'I understand. It depends on the day and the mood, I think.'

'She is so like her mother, God rest her soul.' Simeon sighed. 'Women, they demand much, Señor Vallejo.'

'*Sí, sí,*' replied Diego. 'My Concepción, she thinks she is the circus owner, not me. She is always making demands of me, change this, change that.'

'Much like this silver mine,' Simeon added expansively, gesturing to a collection of buildings up the side of the mountain. All seemed connected by wooden latticework. 'The ore is dug out of that cave near the top of the mountain,' he explained. 'Each building is a different step in the refining process. The ore we mine isn't pure – it's encased in rock, combined with earth. It also contains traces of iron ore and other minerals.'

'I did not know that, *señor.* I thought it was like gold, just ready to be picked up like nuggets!'

Simeon smiled. 'First, it has to be pounded into small fragments.' He pointed to a building from which emitted a grinding noise. 'That's the *arrastra.*'

'*Sí,* I know, a kind of drag-stone mill.'

Simeon seemed surprised. 'You know the process?'

Diego shook his head and grinned. 'No, but the name *arrastra*, it comes from the Spanish *arrastre*, hauling, dragging.'

'Of course – from the Roman process in Spain, no doubt!' Simeon clapped his hands, and pointed at the arrastra building. 'The ore is laid out in a stone pit we've cut into the mountainside. We use mules to turn the grindstone to crush the ore.' He indicated the wooden chute on a trestle sloping down to another area further down. 'There, the fragments are sprayed with mercury, salt and copper sulphate. More mules mix the stuff. A chemical reaction dissolves the silver in the mercury so we get an amalgam of mercury and silver, which is sent down to another stage to be washed off.'

'And that, *señor*?' Diego pointed to a building near the base of the mountain. White smoke or steam erupted from tall tin chimneys.

'The final step for us. The amalgam's heated there to drive off the mercury. What's left is silver, which we smelt into ingots.'

'It is a big undertaking, *señor*.'

Simeon nodded. 'It is. The same method has gone on for over three hundred years.' Simeon bowed, smiled. 'We call it the Mexican process.'

'I like that very much,' said Diego, his chest expanding with national pride. He turned to face the pyramid of silver near the winch building and pointed up the mountain. 'Why have you mined a second place, up there?'

Simeon gestured at a small cave halfway up the mountain. 'That has delivered a rich seam. It's worth sending my best men up there to work on it. They dig out twice the value of all my other men put together, but the conditions are cramped. Sadly, they think it will be short-lived.' He indicated the winch cable. 'It's that pure, it's sent directly to the bottom to be smelted.'

'It's a long way up.'

'So it is. But they get paid extra for the risk.'

Diego pointed past the watchtower. 'And the cartwheel tracks, where do they lead?'

'A sheer drop to Rabbit Creek far below.' As though distracted, Gray gestured vaguely in that direction. 'From there the spoil from the mine is tipped.' He frowned. 'It isn't a pretty sight, but progress demands more and more silver.' He shrugged. 'So we must plunder the land.'

'I see.' Diego had already noted the mass of tree stumps surrounding boot hill. Barely fifty trees remained at the west side of the town. He noted that opposite this balcony was the gully. Then there was another watchtower at this end of the horseshoe.

Diego's chest swelled with a different kind of pride now. On the northern bank of the creek was the common land, presently occupied by the big top and other smaller circus tents. He'd never seen his circus from such a vantage point before. It surely was breathtaking.

Chad Harper woke with a pounding headache and fleetingly wondered where he was. Then he remembered. His room was above the saloon – small, with only a bed, a tallboy, a washbasin, a chair, a single door and two windows. His clothes and a woman's were scattered on the bare boards. Hell, he must have had a good night! Denver sure knew how to entertain a fellow. . . . He felt movement in the bed beside him and turned his throbbing head.

The blonde moved slightly in her sleep, her bare back to him.

He couldn't remember much about last night – save that he'd won at poker and snagged this blonde, climbed the stairs. He was partial to blondes and she'd been available. The rest was a blank. He swore under his breath.

Despite the anvil chorus in his head, he sensed a powerful urge. As he reached a hand out to grasp her shoulder and turn her to him, he was baulked by heavy knocking on the door. He sat up, barked, 'Who is it? What do you want?' He instantly regretted shouting, as his head throbbed anew.

'Telegram for you, sir!' The voice behind the door was tremulous.

'For me? Can't it wait?'

'Sender says it's urgent, sir. Sorry, sir.'

Tumbling out of bed, the bedsprings creaking, Chad glanced at the woman. She moaned but otherwise didn't register his movement. Naked, he padded to the door, unlocked it and opened it.

A gaunt telegraph man trembled on the threshold, his bespectacled eyes darting, making a conscious effort not to look anywhere but Chad's face. 'There's no reply, sir, but I had to deliver it at once, and personally.' He licked his lips, eyes lighting up as he glimpsed the woman in the bed.

Chad scratched his chest hair, took the flimsy yellow paper. 'I'd give you a tip, but I'm outta pockets right now.'

'That's all right, sir. I've done what's required.' The man turned on his heel and hurried along the landing to the head of the stairs.

Leaning against the doorpost, Chad read the message: *Meet me at Mesita with your men. Hart.*

His headache seemed to ease at those words and what they promised. He smiled. Yes, he could round up Marvin and Trampas. He glanced over his shoulder as the blonde sat up, sleepily wiping her eyes.

First, he had something to do – and this time he'd remember every blessed minute of it. Damn, but he felt sure women would be the death of him one day.

Now, as the circus thrived, Diego Vallejo was no longer welcome in the office of Simeon Gray.

Simeon stood on the office balcony and fumed. He'd been told by the town gossip, of all people – Rosanna Dent, the restaurant owner – that his daughter Naomi was seeing too much of one of the circus performers. He supposed she was ripe for a wedding, at seventeen – granted, he'd married Edith when she was only eighteen – but he was damned if he'd condone his daughter going off to a life in the circus!

He berated himself. It was only idle gossip. Probably nothing in it. He'd question Naomi over dinner – at the Dent woman's restaurant; that should silence her gossip!

On the circus's first show night, at the close of the performances, Naomi rushed out of the big tent and accosted Antonio the sharpshooter, praising him on his skill.

'Thank you kindly, Miss. Although they're the tools of my trade, I hold them in high esteem and great respect – much like young ladies of my acquaintance.' He bowed extravagantly and reached out for her hand.

'Oh, goodness,' Naomi quailed.

'Naomi! Come here at once!' Simeon Gray stormed up to the pair. 'Unhand my daughter, sir, at once!'

'Surely, sir.' Antonio let her hand drop. 'We were just passing the time of day, sir. Nothing more.'

Growling his displeasure, Simeon grabbed Naomi's arm. 'Come, child, we're going home and we won't be coming to the circus again – ever!'

The next day, on her way to work at the general store, Naomi took a slight detour. She was watched by Emmett Rosco, who spent his time around the circus wagons and animal cages.

Naomi handed Antonio a note.

Intrigued, Emmett watched as Naomi ran off. Antonio the sharpshooter read the note, smiled, then grinned and crumpled the sheet of paper into a ball and threw it on the grass. A short while later, Emmett retrieved the ball of paper and read the scrawled words: *Meet me at the shoe-smith tomorrow morning.*

This was so exciting! Emmett dragged along his best friend Gene Tubbs. Gene was almost a foot taller, six months older and big-boned like his pa, but he deferred to Emmett's quick wits and sharp mind. They both watched as Antonio and Naomi's secret flirtation began, first with a few stolen kisses behind the newspaper offices, overlooking the road to boot hill. Thereafter, Emmett and Gene decided that it wasn't so exciting after all and went back to the sideshows. Gene was agog.

'There's so many things, so many tricks, it's enough to boggle the mind!' he wailed.

'I'm not interested,' Emmett said. 'I prefer the escapologist and the sharpshooter; that's what I want to do when I'm older.'

Gene scratched his flat nose. 'Seems to me the sharp-shooter's good with his sharp tongue as well as his six-gun!'

'I'm not interested in girls, Gene – not for a while, anyways.' He ruffled Gene's dark brown hair. 'Pa says it'll happen one day, I'll just want to be with a girl rather than with my best pal.'

'Yeah, my pa says the same. Can't figure it, though.'

They both made their secret sign and shook hands in their special way. 'Together, forever!'

As they quietened down, Gene said, 'Anyway, your pa's a pretty good shot with his six-gun. He don't have to follow no circus.'

Emmett nodded, and grinned. 'Yeah, he is. The town's a safer place with him at the helm.'

'I thought that a helm belonged on a ship, not a town.'

'Well, it's sort of the same. You know what I mean!'

'Yeah, it's plain sailing with Sheriff Rosco in charge!'

Emmett clapped his friend on the back. 'You got it right, Gene! Pa says we welcome the circus and we'll benefit . . . somehow.'

'Maybe,' Gene said wistfully. 'I reckon Naomi Gray's pretty welcoming to the circus, don't you?'

Not everyone in town was so hospitable, as Sheriff Tad Rosco learned. Only last night Ignacio Bandini was in a fight with a townsman over horses. It was obvious by his language and

23

demeanour that the man – Shanley Donnelly – hated Mexicans and Indians. As he was the chief engineer of the mine, he held sway over many townspeople, while Bandini was just a foreign visitor. Still, Sheriff Rosco jailed the pair of them for the night – in separate cells. When he called the circus owner in, Diego Vallejo informed him that, fortunately, 'Ignacio can nurse his bruises and his pride without embarrassment. As the circus wrangler, he doesn't have to appear in public.'

Sheriff Rosco shrugged. 'I'm sorry I can't do anything. A witness says that Donnelly started the fight, but he's outnumbered by others – fellow miners, in fact – who blame your man.'

'I am a man of the world, Sheriff. I know how things are north of the border.'

'We're not all like that, Señor Vallejo.'

'I am sure you are not. But I know your hands are tied.'

'You're one astute circus owner, *señor*.'

'Indeed, thank you, Sheriff. I know the mine owns the town in all but deeds.'

Sheriff Rosco made a faint-hearted attempt to deny the damning statement, but the denial stuck in his craw.

Now, some days later, Diego was glad that their stay would end tonight. Straight after the show, they'd begin dismantling the booths and seats and finish hauling down the big tent first thing in the morning.

The circus was due in at Mesita for their first show tomorrow evening. Mesita was a slightly larger town and would, he hoped, bring in more money, even though they were only scheduled to stay until Tuesday. As ever, he wasn't sure about the reception his people would receive. It was ever thus, north of the border.

CHAPTER 2

NOT A DAY OF REST

Saturday

Twelve riders converged on the crossroads that merged with the approach road to Mesita. They reined to a halt. The dust settled.

Lee Grant, feeling comfortable, since he was backed up by Chip, Vince and Bernie, withdrew his hat, dried the sweat from his forehead with a sleeve. 'Howdy. Heading for Mesita?'

'Yeah, what of it?' grated Mack Calhoun.

'So are we – but what's it to you, mister?' said Chad Harper.

Grant grinned. 'Way I see it, Hart called you all to meet him at Mesita.'

Calhoun eyed Grant, then Chad. 'Is that right?'

'Aye,' said Chad, 'true enough. It sounds like whatever Hart's got planned, it's big – and needs plenty of good guns.'

'Name's Grant, Lee Grant,' he said, offering his hand.

Calhoun eased his horse alongside Grant's, shook, and introduced himself.

Chad took off his hat, wiped the band. 'Chad, Chad Harper.' He chuckled then spat dust on to the ground. 'Hart and me go way back, how about you guys?'

'I know Hart – he's a man of his word,' said Grant. 'That's all you need to be aware of.'

'Yeah,' Calhoun added, 'we work *with* Hart, remember that, not *for* him.'

'Sure, sure.' Chad nodded. 'I'm sure there'll be enough to share,' he said, turning in his creaking saddle, eyeing all of them.

'I don't know about you guys, but I need a drink!' Grant spurred his mount forward. The rest followed at a steady pace, several men exchanging monikers as they went.

Roger Hart studied the three men and a woman who lounged in chairs in the back room of the Last Chance, the only saloon in Mesita. They didn't know it yet, but these next few weeks would change all their lives forever. He smiled at his girl Emily Chase, who sat next to him; opposite sat Heath Kendall, ex-sergeant, faithful friend and right-arm man when Hart was a Confederate lieutenant. He'd recruited Theo Leese two weeks ago; the man was a hard villain, a bank robber, but he was needed for another reason. Theo had trained briefly to work on the telegraph. Bret Pike was hired for a good reason too – the man was an explosives expert, wanted for six murders at a gold mine. Hart grunted, noting the whiskey bottle and the five glasses on the table were empty. Birds chirped outside the only window that opened on to an area of waste ground; this building was at the edge of the town.

Hart turned to Emily Chase. Her split leather riding skirt revealed a tantalizing glimpse of flesh above her scuffed boots. Her sombrero hung on her back, held by a leather cord round her delicate throat. 'Get some more redeye, honey, I'm parched.'

'Sure, Roger.' She gave him a smile with sensual lips, tossed her flaxen hair and stood up, straightening her skirt. She was about to move to the door but stopped, nodded at the open window. 'I can hear horsemen – a lot of them – coming fast. Trouble?'

Hart shook his head. 'No worries, they're men I've been recruiting.'

Emily pouted. 'You never told me that.'

Bret said, 'You didn't tell us, neither.' He gestured at Theo.

'Slipped our minds is all,' said Heath Kendall.

Hart smacked Emily's behind. 'Still here? Go get the liquor.'

She flounced out and the other three men chuckled.

Emily stood at the door, her mouth twisting as she listened. Sometimes, she wondered why she stayed with Roger. He could be so – so annoying. She rubbed her behind. Why'd she always get landed with no-good men? Because she liked what they provided, probably. . . .

Maybe once this big job was over, maybe they could settle down respectable-like. But would she cotton to that, really? Her life had been hard – tough, even – for years. Respectable just could be a mite boring.

Still, she owed Roger. When she'd escaped that bordello in New Mexico, she'd been wandering in the desert for what seemed like days. It was probably only a day, but it seemed longer. And Roger had found her. He'd seemed heaven-sent, all six-two of him, his skin the colour of burlap. He'd studied her with those wide-set steel-grey eyes while he gave her water. She'd made up a story to explain her being abandoned by an ingrate family, and he'd bought it. He'd been concerned, gentle, his voice resonant – in fact he reminded her of José. She shook her head. José was the only customer she'd been partial to in the bordello; he'd seemed genuinely to like her for who she was, not what she was. But she couldn't abide his smell – he always stank of horseflesh. His job, he said; it brought in the money – money he spent on her. She would've stayed for him, but he moved on after two weeks – probably to corral another filly. It had been a heady two weeks, though, and he'd paid her well for her attention.

Then, the next day after José's departure, things got ugly with a cowpoke who didn't know how to behave. Maybe she'd been spoiled by José. No matter, the madam took the side of the cowpoke, so she decided to get out while she could. Stupidly, not wanting to risk being lynched as a horse-thief, she'd set off on foot. And promptly got lost.

Yeah, Roger doubtless saved my life, she reckoned. Pity he couldn't show a little more respect, though.

'How old is she?' Theo asked in his reedy voice, thumbing at the door. His brown hair was close-cropped, his complexion doughy, probably due to the fact he'd spent half of his two dozen years in prison.

'Says she's nineteen,' Hart said, smiling, 'but acts a whole lot older, I can assure you.'

Brushing a hand over his skewed nose and boxcar moustache, Theo asked, 'Where'd you meet up?'

'You seem all-fired interested in her all of a sudden,' Hart growled. 'Should I be worried?'

'No, no, of course not.' Theo cleared his throat and his voice altered, concern in his tone. 'So why'd we want to recruit more men – and how many, for God's sake?'

'There'll be enough loot to go around, even if we hire thirty or more.'

'Thirty!' Bret bellowed. He had an explosive temperament and his appearance seemed to reinforce this: freckled faced, red hair, razor-burned neck and ginger stubble on chin and jaw. He wasn't a tall man, barely five-six, but he had a rugged body and piercing Nordic blue eyes that could cut people cold.

'You didn't answer me,' persisted Theo. 'Why'd we need thirty?'

Hart shrugged. 'It's enough to hold a town, that's why.'

Theo whistled. 'A town?'

Bret said, 'What town?'

'Conejos Blancos.' Hart grinned.

'That's west a ways.' Bret scratched his head. Now he spoke more than a few words, his nasal twang was obvious and a little annoying. Hart shrugged; he'd get used to it. 'Why do we need to hold the town?'

'There's a silver mine just next to it,' Kendall said, his voice tobacco-roughened. His dusty, road-coloured eyes sparkled as he added, 'We're going to take over the mine, as well.'

Theo whistled.

'And,' said Hart, 'get all that ore the miners dig up in two weeks.'

Bret gaped. 'Two weeks? That's a long time to control a town – and the mine!'

'We'll be taking hostages,' Hart said, 'so they'll all comply with our wishes. When we're done, we'll let them go. They'll be grateful.'

'But the town,' said Theo, 'once we let them go, they'll get a posse together, they'll—'

'What's it to the townsfolk?' Kendall snapped. 'It's the mine owner who loses out, not the town.'

Theo nodded, chuckling. 'Sure, it's not as if there ain't enough silver in the ground. They just have to dig up more, after we've skedaddled.'

'That's the general idea,' Hart said.

Outside, the sound of horses' hoofs stopped.

Hart said, 'Our gang's just about to get bigger – a whole lot bigger.'

'Thirty – seems a lot to share with,' Bret whispered.

'There's more than enough to go round, believe me,' said Hart. 'Once we've got our gang organized, we'll hit the town tomorrow.'

'I can hardly wait,' said Kendall.

'Sunday.' Theo grinned. 'Praise be to the Lord! Then we'll be mine owners!'

Twelve dust-stained men entered the Last Chance Saloon. 'We need a drink,' said the husky man in front, eyeing the barkeep. An attractive blonde in a split riding skirt was fondling two whiskey bottles on the customers' side of the counter.

'Coming right up, sir!'

'Where's Hart?' the husky man demanded.

'In the back room, sir.'

'Tell him Chad Harper and a few others are here.' Husky grabbed the proffered whiskey bottle.

'Tell him yourself,' the blonde said. 'The bartender ain't a messenger. He tends bar.'

Chad eyed her. 'You join me later, blondie?' he growled.

'Name ain't blondie, it's Emily. Emily Chase. Sorry, I'm taken.'

'Oh, I'm sure I can come to some arrangement with the guy.'

'I don't think so,' Emily said. 'My guy is Hart, the man you want to see.' She moved away from the counter with the two bottles of whiskey.

'OK, honey,' Chad said, following her. 'I like what you're packing, and I don't mean the liquor.'

'You can look but don't touch,' she said and opened the door to the back room. 'Roger, you've got company,' she said and stepped inside.

Chad followed and studied those assembled. 'What kind of circus is this, anyway?'

*

The circus paraded into Mesita and after much fanfare and boisterous haranguing of the populace, they set up the big top just outside the town.

As he watched, Bret said, 'I'm looking forward to this evening. I fancy my chances at the stalls!'

'Spend your money if you want,' Hart said. 'But remember, nobody drinks tonight! We don't want any trouble. We ride first thing tomorrow and we'll meet up with the rest of the gang outside Conejos Blancos.'

Theo laughed over the dog in its colourful ruff as it performed tricks, while Bret cowered whenever the huge lion snarled at its brave chair-wielding trainer, Reginaldo in his grey and red tunic.

All of them were awed by the strength of the man called Hercules del Valle, with his barrel chest, rippling muscles and leopard-skin trunks.

Sunday

Dressed in his best clothes, Emmett Rosco sat at the table in Dent's Eatery, opposite his ma and pa. The restaurant was three-quarters full with townspeople breakfasting before going to church. Mrs Dent always did well on a Sunday; she was forever saying it wasn't a day of rest for her, while she counted the money. He flushed hotly as he felt the eyes of other diners on him and his pa. No matter how often he was with Pa, he noticed that people treated him differently – because he was the sheriff's son. Pa was a highly respected citizen, that's what they said, and he looked the part in his pinstripe suit, vest and shining black boots. Emmett's eyes darted from his father's gold star to the holstered pearl-handled Smith & Wesson .45. One day, maybe he'd be a sheriff – or even a marshal – and tame the West.

'Eat your eggs, Emmett,' Ma scolded.

'Yes, Ma.'

Then his gaze was drawn to the door as the overhead bell tinkled. Two dust-covered men entered, one rangy and dark-skinned, the other stout and sporting a face full of hair. They removed their hats and slapped them against their thighs to dislodge dust from their clothes.

'Hey, we want some grub – and pretty darn quick!' said the lanky one. 'We've ridden a long way!'

Mrs Dent paused in her serving of Widow McKenzie, the owner of the general store. 'Go out back and wash off that trail dust.' She brushed aside a stray tendril of brunette hair, raised her head, looking down her nose at them, her high-cut nostrils flaring. '*Then* I'll consider serving you!'

The bearded man laughed. 'She don't take kindly to you, Pat,' he said, nudging his partner, and pulled up a chair at a vacant table. The lanky one swore under his breath and sat. They put their hats on the far side of the table.

Emmett noticed they both wore gun-belts, their six-guns dulled with over-use. And the room suddenly went very quiet; others had noticed, too. He felt a chill run down his spine. The man called Pat scowled. 'Just bring the food, bitch, and be quick about it!'

There was a gasp or two from the seated women. Alice, one of Emmett's school-friends, started to weep.

Mrs Dent took a step forward, her normally peachy complexion now beetroot red, a scowl creasing her features.

Emmett noticed the glance of concern that passed from Ma to Pa. He shook his head slightly and stood up, eased back his chair. He took a couple of paces, reached out an arm and steadied Mrs Dent. Some unspoken words passed between them, Emmett reckoned. And then Pa turned and hitched his gun-belt on his hip. He looked so commanding, standing there in his Sunday best.

'It's clear to me that you don't like doing what you're told,' Pa said to the two men. 'The sign at the entrance to town says hand in your weapons.' He walked up to their table.

The pair shoved back their chairs and stood, eyes narrowed.

'Pat, we've got unwanted company,' said the lanky one.

'Hey, Coburn, this sheriff's been eating too much pie!' He pointed to Pa's belly overlapping his gun-belt.

Emmett blushed in embarrassment; he'd never really noticed before.

'Maybe, but that don't make me soft,' Pa grated. He held out a hand. 'Just take out your weapons, nice and easy, butt first.'

Coburn did, careful to hold the revolver by the barrel.

'Mine, as well, Sheriff?' asked Pat.

When Pa turned to Pat, Coburn slammed the butt of his pistol against Pa's temple.

Emmett rose from the table, his insides doing all sorts of things as Pa stumbled.

The man called Pat drew his Colt and fired at Pa almost point blank. The shot seemed deafening in the hushed room.

Ma let out a sharp cry and pushed her chair back, instinctively reaching for Emmett's shoulder. 'Oh, what have you done?'

'He was going for his gun!' Pat shouted, waving his smoking pistol.

Emmett shrugged off Ma's hand and ran. 'Pa!' He sank to his knees and then glared up at the man called Pat. 'You're a liar! Pa never went for his gun!'

Pat cocked his Colt, levelled it at Emmett.

Suddenly, Emmett's world shrank to the size of that black hole at the end of the gun-barrel. He felt his bladder threaten to burst but by force of will he contained it, all the while his heart hammering loudly against his chest. He stared, realizing that maybe being a lawman wasn't going to be his lot – nothing was, now; he was going to die!

Ma shrieked and rushed forward, her skirts swishing. 'He's an unarmed boy!' she snarled. She seemed like a wildcat at bay. 'Leave him be!'

The two men picked up their hats and Coburn said, 'I've lost my appetite anyway. Let's go.'

The pair left, the doorbell jangling.

Next door at McGee's Hotel, Mayor Carl Travis was dressed for church in his charcoal grey suit, waistcoat, black shoes and white silk shirt. It was a regular event he had established, to pop into the hotel and study the account book. His wife Lucy knew where he was and, considering his whiskey nose, she probably guessed he imbibed in a good measure at each visit. His sallow complexion paled when he heard the shot. He turned to the manager, whose face reflected his own sudden alarm, and then slammed the book shut and rushed out.

On his way he passed two dust-covered strangers who strode along the boardwalk in a leisurely fashion, then mounted their nags and rode at a sedate pace towards the southern end of town.

He entered the eatery. It was pandemonium. He first noticed Rosanna standing beside a table, which she held on to for support, her face pale, eyes distraught. Several customers stared, white-faced, at the kneeling form of Hayley Rosco and her son Emmett, huddled over the body of the sheriff, their Sunday best clothes blood-stained. Beside them stood a bald man with a bulbous nose and a horseshoe-grey moustache, Nevin Ulrich, the town's doctor.

He eyed the doctor and Ulrich shook his head. 'We all saw it, two strangers – one of them gunned down Tad. He didn't have a chance.'

Travis blanched as he realized he'd probably walked past the killer on his way here. And poor Hayley and her son had witnessed the murder. His insides churned and he felt queasy. He

34

wanted to sit down. Violence didn't set well with him. But he had to pull himself together, as the eyes of many turned on him for guidance. He should act decisively, but he felt incapable of coherent thought, his legs unable to move.

At that moment Deputy Sheriff Dan Leavy hurried in, his six-gun drawn. He was lean, tall and yet diffident, often a foil for the sheriff's bluster, by all accounts. He took in the scene with a swift glance and swore, quickly apologized to the ladies present, then added, 'Mayor, I need to organize a posse of four men. Help me do that, will you?'

Travis emerged from his mind-numbing trance, nodded and sensed movement in his legs. 'Yes. . . .' He glanced round the room. 'Has anyone sent for Virgil?'

'Yeah, my wife went,' Doc Ulrich said.

'They rode out of town, heading south,' Travis told Leavy. 'You should catch up with them if you go now.'

The posse was long gone. It was mid-morning by the time undertaker, Virgil Perry, had the sheriff in a box on a sawhorse before the church dais. Standing to one side, Perry held himself in a respectful pose, his obsidian eyes scanning the congregation, as if sizing them all up for future work. He rubbed his aquiline nose with the silver handle of his walking stick.

In the front pew knelt Emmett and his ma, their faces blotchy red and streaked with tears.

By now the church was crowded, the subdued sound a mixture of prayers and sobbing.

Standing to one side of the coffin, the rotund Reverend Christie intoned, 'May the Lord guide our posse of townsmen to capture the two evil men who committed this despicable act and bring them to swift justice and retribution, Amen!'

The responding 'Amens' seemed almost to lift off the roof of the church.

CHAPTER 3

TOWN CLOSED

They rode in from the south. Hart's men were bunched to either side of him. He reined in at the town sign proclaiming Conejos Blancos had a population of 268. Below it another notice announced the ordnance law of the town: all weapons must be surrendered to the sheriff on arrival.

'Not today,' Hart mused. He leaned on his saddle horn and glanced at the others.

Three men sat on their horses with their hands tied behind their backs; two posse riders had died in the shootout on the trail and Hart hadn't lost a single man. He eyed Greg Wilkins who drove the empty buckboard and signed for them all to move.

Then he led them on, past the smithy and tannery. A few paces later, he heard what sounded like the prayers – lots of 'Amens', anyway – from the church on their left. He raised an arm and they all drew rein, thirty-nine riders and one buckboard driver.

From here Hart could see down the full length of Main Street. Just as Pat described, Dent's Livery was over on his right, opposite the church entrance steps, but it appeared unattended. On the opposite corner of the western block, there was the printer's, then Dent's Eatery. He idly wondered if Dent owned the town; well, if he did, it wouldn't be for much longer.

The streets were empty of people; the place was like a ghost town. He turned in his saddle, the leather creaking, and eyed Pat and Coburn. 'Pat, you did us a favour. Got rid of the lawman and crammed the church with most of the townsfolk.'

'Glad to oblige,' said Pat, and grinned.

Hart glanced at the three captives and the rider beside them. 'Theo, take what's left of this sorry posse to the cells.' He nodded at the rest of his men. 'You know what to do. Go to it.'

Leaning on his saddle-horn, Hart watched with satisfaction as his men did his bidding. Even the other gang leaders, Calhoun and Grant, didn't seem to mind him taking charge. He hoped that would last.

Their horses at a slow canter, Theo and Greg led the three captives down Main Street, eyes watchful on both sides. Two-thirds down, they turned their horses to the left and halted, dismounting outside the sheriff's office.

Birds chirped. Somewhere a dog barked.

Prayers still filled the church.

Everything normal. But not for much longer.

Now, several men led by Calhoun fanned out on horseback, four veering east along Hallahan Road towards the junction with North Street that ran parallel with Main. They dismounted and stood outside the funeral parlour. Hart wondered how much work the undertaker would get over the next few days, until the townspeople were suitably cowed. Four more men dismounted at the printer's and the shoe-smith opposite.

Eight men led by Grant rode quietly down Main Street and stationed themselves outside the town hall steps at the end of the thoroughfare. These eight would cover the north end of town, in case anyone had ideas of running that way.

Kendall and seven others rode to the left, along Hallahan and turned right into West Street. They rode past a forested area on their left, where many trees had already been felled, then past boot hill on a slight incline at the foot of the mountain that loomed. Ahead, they followed the dirt road that veered towards the left and approached the entrance of the silver mine, blocked by two tall wooden gates, chained and pad-locked. The two watch towers were not manned during the day.

A man stepped out from a shed at the side of the road, a Greener in the crook of his arm. 'We don't open Sundays, stranger. If you want the boss, he's at church.'

'No,' Kendall said, 'we don't want the boss. We want the mine.'

'What the hell, you say?' He raised the weapon.

Kendall spurred his mount forward, its flank shoving the man over. Bret came at the man from the other side, slammed a rifle butt against his cranium. He collapsed like a sack of potatoes. Bret slid off his horse, ransacked the man's pockets and then grinned, holding up a bunch of keys. He hurried over to the gate and unlocked the padlocks.

Not a shot had been fired so far, and now they had taken the mine.

Theo locked their captives in the jail and then the pair moved down the left-hand-side-covered veranda, past the lawyer's office to the building that housed the telegraph office, the stage depot and the mine offices.

Pistol drawn, Greg kicked open the door. A counter for cus-tomers and beyond that the telegrapher's desk, which was unmanned.

'Just fine,' Theo said. He quickly scoured the room. Over on the left was a curtained-off section. He pulled back the wool drape to reveal a stack of boxes and crates, each labelled with destinations: Colorado Springs, Denver, Alamosa. . . On the right of this partitioned area was another counter. A sign hung over it: Left Luggage. 'Check upstairs.'

Greg nodded and hurried up, two stairs at a time.

Theo replaced his gun in its holster, returned to the desk and examined the apparatus. It had been a while, but he was familiar with it. Sure, he was a mite rusty, but he should still be able to send and receive messages, which was what Hart was banking on, in an attempt at keeping the lid on the town's takeover.

Greg called down, 'No one's at home!'

Theo grinned. 'They are now.' He removed his jacket, draped it on the chair, rolled up his sleeves and sat at the desk.

The men at the southern end of town accompanied the buckboard driver. Thanks to the information Pat supplied, Hart reasoned that since nobody was allowed to carry arms in the town, the weapons must be kept indoors, so now they methodically went from building to building, locating any guns, stacking them in the buckboard as they went.

Hart stationed two men at the back door of the church and one at the meeting room adjacent. That left him with Emily, Pat and Coburn, their six-guns drawn. He opened the church doors.

The church was indeed full – standing room only. A few people near the doors turned their heads at the intrusion and their faces paled. Hart couldn't blame them.

Hart grabbed a woman in the rear group. A woman standing next to her whispered, 'Shelly, oh, my God!'

'I'll be all right,' Shelly replied, her voice faint and weak with fear, belying her words.

Hart shoved her ahead of him, down the aisle, and as they passed some people stopped singing and gasped in alarm; men's voices were raised.

The prayers stumbled to a halt.

Reverend Christie lowered his Bible and his jowl wobbled. 'What is the meaning of this intrusion? You shouldn't be carrying weapons in the house of the Lord!'

Hart fired a shot into the wood ceiling; splinters fell, exclamations erupted. 'I'm taking over your town for a little while, folks.'

A few voices began to chatter, many in disbelief.

Waving his pistol, Hart added, 'No need to be alarmed.' He gripped Shelly's arm, shook her violently. 'Do as we ask of you and no one will get hurt!'

'But what do you want?' persisted Reverend Christie.

'We're going to hold some of you hostage. The rest of you will go about your normal daily business. Anyone tries to leave town or fight – and I mean anyone! – and I start killing hostages.'

Reverend Christie looked at the hole in the ceiling, or maybe to heaven, then asked, 'How long is this going to go on for?'

'Two weeks.'

More gasps.

'Impossible!' the priest exclaimed.

'Make it possible, Reverend.' Hart eyed the congregation. 'Some of you might think I'm bluffing, so I'll show you now that I ain't.' He cocked his pistol and aimed it at Shelly's temple.

She closed her eyes and trembled in his grip.

'Wait!' On the right, a woman with a wan complexion stepped out from the front pew. She wore black – a widow's weeds. She had a firm mouth, dove grey eyes and auburn hair.

'Who are you?' Hart sneered. 'The town mayor?'

'My name's Lily McKenzie.' She took another step forward. 'Why take this young woman's life – she has lots to live for. Mine is all but over, so take mine, if you must. But spare hers.'

Hart let go briefly, then snatched at Shelly's hair, rubbed the snout of his six-gun over her lipstick, smearing it. 'She's a painted lady, so no great loss.' He levelled his gun.

'She's here worshipping the Lord.' Lily turned to face the congregation. 'As are we all.'

Hart pointed the gun at Lily. 'If you ain't the mayor, what do you do?'

'The general store is mine. I run it in my late husband's stead.'

Hart laughed. 'Well, there you are, then. You're useful to the town – so you get to live.' He turned to Shelly.

Shelly closed her eyes and whispered prayers through her smudged lips.

Abruptly, Hart jerked to face the worshippers and fired at the front rank on his left, at a woman who clasped the arm of her man. He let go of Shelly. 'You're reprieved, dove.'

'Oh, my God,' Lily exclaimed, running over, 'you've shot the doctor's wife!'

'Well, ain't she the lucky one?'

Doc Ulrich knelt by his wife, Mary. He looked up, his eyes burning. 'You heartless bastard!'

'Nope, that ain't me, since the name's Hart. I'm full of heart, you might say.' He laughed. 'OK. No more heroics. Looks like the doc's wife might live.' He shrugged. 'Next time, my aim won't be off.' He gestured towards Pat. 'Just oblige my trigger-happy friend here and give your names and occupations, if any.'

A few women sobbed and a couple of men whimpered. Hart ignored them. 'Until I give new orders, you're all to stay here!

41

Is that understood?'

Some responded with docile yesses, others stayed silent, either insolent or fearful. Hart didn't care; for now, they were cowed.

Emmett recognized the man with the leader. Pat was his name; the cur that killed Pa. Fierce burning hate reddened his face and he clenched his fists. He glanced up at Ma. She didn't seem to know or care what was happening; she only had eyes for Pa's coffin.

Reverend Christie stepped forward and placed a hand on Ma's trembling shoulder. In a firm voice, he addressed Hart: 'We need to bury our sheriff.'

Hart glared then shrugged. 'You're right, Padre.' He glanced over his shoulder. 'By rights, Pat, you should go, since you killed him.'

Pat shrugged, as if he didn't particularly care one way or the other.

Hart grinned. 'Anyway, you did us a favour, so, Coburn, you go with the priest and pick four pallbearers. Only take the widow.' He scanned the room. 'Nobody else attends the funeral, you hear?'

A few nodded, and one or two mumbled responses.

Emmett clasped Ma's hand tightly.

'Yeah, OK, the kid can go and bury his pa,' Hart conceded. 'When he's in the ground, Coburn, join the search for weapons.'

'Aye, boss.'

Hart turned to Emily. 'Pat and I can handle them here – you go and search for weapons as well.'

The small funeral procession climbed down the church steps, turned left along Hallahan Road, and then right up West Street. They moved at a quick pace and Emmett almost had to jog to stay with them. Through the haze of tears he saw the entrance to boot hill on the left.

A short hard path inclined up to the cemetery area and beyond the white picket fence posts he saw the familiar assortment of wood and stone grave markers. The number of times he'd passed here and never once had he contemplated laying his pa to rest. His chest ached fit to burst. He tried in vain to blink back the tears; it was as if a flood was erupting from his heaving pained heart and exiting through his eyes, unending.

As arranged, Hart received reports from his men and it seemed that everything went smoothly.

The saloon owner Alden Tubbs was still behind the bar of the Rabbit's Hole when Calhoun's men entered. His shotgun was promptly confiscated. Two men climbed the stairs and checked the rooms. Only a couple were occupied – by miners, sleeping off drink. Neither carried any weapon.

In The Passion Flower bordello, there were no customers, only the Madame, Helen Larkin, and seven girls. Their initial surprise, expecting paying customers, swiftly turned to displeasure when they were herded into the downstairs salon and told to sit and wait for instructions. Four derringers were found in thigh garters, much to the amusement of the searchers. 'We'll try the merchandise later, ladies,' promised one of the men whose name was Chad.

They located Simeon Gray with his daughter Naomi at home in their row house at the end of North Street. He reluctantly surrendered his six-gun and vociferously objected when the woman Emily Chase searched Naomi for a weapon. The barber and his wife clearly were not religious and were found in bed when Hart's men burst in; they had no weapons, though the woman attempted to use the chamber pot to brain one of the intruders; he got a face full of piss and she suffered a broken nose in retaliation. The shoe-smith and his wife were busy checking inventory and didn't put up a fight; he docilely handed over his shotgun. Dent, the livery man, surrendered a pistol from his drawer.

Soon, the bed of the buckboard was stacked with weapons.

While this went on, Bret Pike spent his time laying and wiring explosives round the town hall, locating the fuses at the rear, out of sight.

It soon became obvious that the children were not considered a threat to the men who had taken over the town. Emmett left his ma in her bedroom, grief-stricken; there was nothing he could do for her right now. So he sought out his best friend Gene and the pair watched as the rest of the worshippers were railroaded out of the church. The people were broken up into groups. Emmett spotted some other school friends milling around.

'Quick,' urged Emmett, 'we need to know where they're all being taken!'

'Sure.' Gene hastily approached two girls and another boy – Alice, Maura and Eric – while their parents and others were escorted to different destinations around the town.

Standing on the corner of the newspaper and printer's office, Maura asked, 'Why must we spy on them?'

'If we're going to help our parents,' Emmett said, gesturing at the groups being led away, 'we need to know where they're being held and what they're doing, don't we?'

'But how can we help them?' asked Eric. 'We're only kids.'

'Knowledge is power,' opined Alice, flicking her honey-blonde hair back and folding her arms smugly.

'Alice is right,' whispered Maura. 'If we can get help somehow, we need to know as much as we can.'

'Exactly!' Emmett said. 'Let's split up and we'll all report back at the livery.'

By the end of the day, the children had learned most of the names of the men who had taken over the town, and where the hostages were held.

Emmett spun a metal hoop towards the town hall, where he pretended to retrieve it. Then he moved to the side of the building and heaved a water butt near a window, climbed on to it and listened.

With patience, he learned that Mayor Travis and his wife Lucy were held here, which seemed appropriate, he supposed. He found out that the mayor's assistant, Mansfield Atkins, had been ordered to run messages considered necessary by Hart between the various hostage buildings. It occurred to him that maybe he could intercept Mr Atkins sometime and get some inside information or gossip about the leader. Then he dismissed the idea; Mr Atkins was a sour cuss and wouldn't bother with the likes of a kid.

Locked in with the mayor were Shelly, the pretty woman Hart first threatened in the church, the wives of the smithy, the baker and the butcher and two other women Emmett didn't rightly know.

He listened at the rear window as concerns were expressed about the lavatory arrangements and the supply of food and drink. Hart snapped that he'd thought of it and everything would be sorted out 'in good time'.

Bret Pike was put on guard at the town hall steps. Emmett gulped when he heard Pike say that he was all ready to ignite the explosives, if there was any 'uprising of the populace'.

Hart left the town hall and strode along Main Street toward the mine entrance. Gene followed him, hiding in the bulrushes and weeds that skirted the roadside on the right. He wasn't able to get into the mine compound, but he overheard the sentry at the gate chatting and learned that Mr Gray and his

45

daughter had been forcibly taken to the office, along with Janet McTavish, the wife of the chief of mining, plus the spouse of the shoe-smith and four townsmen.

It seemed that the one called Hart was going to be stationed here at the mine, in Mr Gray's office. With his woman, Emily. The sentry had a few words to say about Emily Chase. 'I'd chase her any day. She'd enjoy it when I caught her!'

The other sentry laughed and the coarse sound made Gene shiver.

Alice slunk up to the open side window of The Passion Flower and flushed when she spotted Miss Helen Larkin standing with hands on hips. This was the first time she'd been so close to the lady of this house. Her ma rarely spoke about Miss Larkin, and on the odd occasion that her name was mentioned it was always accompanied by a terrible sneer. Apparently, Miss Larkin was a 'scarlet woman' – though Alice thought she looked quite normal, with a full figure and attractive titian hair; maybe Ma didn't know the difference between titian and scarlet?

There were a good number of people in the big salon. Alice counted seven finely dressed ladies, two of whom were nursing Dr Ulrich's wife, Mary, who lay on a couch. None of these women seemed unpleasant, rather considerate, in fact, though they seemed different, with unusually red cheeks and bright red lips.

Squinting round the brocade curtain, she noticed that Matt the telegrapher sat on a plush seat. His eyes were wide, staring at the fine ladies, and didn't seem to notice the four other women sitting on chairs around the walls, which wasn't surprising, Alice thought, since they all looked quite dowdy compared to the painted ladies.

The guard at the door called himself Chad and he seemed to like the look of the colourful ladies, judging by his wide grin.

Eric felt the blood surge as he pulled up a couple of soapboxes and placed them against the brick wall. He climbed on top and peered between the bars of the jail at the rear of the building. This was the most exciting thing that had ever happened in Conejos Blancos – ever! Well, as far as he knew. Sure, there were stories about Indians and shootouts, but that was before he was born.

As he listened, it seemed that nobody spoke quietly; they all shouted. There was a lot of anger, which seemed familiar since his parents were always arguing.

He learned that Deputy Sheriff Dan Leavy was locked behind bars with two other townsmen Eric didn't know.

Through the open door to the jail section, stacked up in the centre of the sheriff's office, he spotted piles and piles of the towns-folks' weapons. Involuntarily, he ground his teeth. How could the town fight back when they had no guns? These intruders seemed clever as well as nasty.

Eric glimpsed over to the right. In a separate cell stood Monty Blake, a notorious killer and bank robber, who brave Sheriff Rosco had cornered and arrested. The circuit judge was due in town soon to set up a court of justice. That, too, seemed exciting, at the time.

Now, he listened as Blake pleaded, 'Come on, let me out! I can be really useful to you guys.'

Then the man called Pat stepped into view and gripped the bars.

Eric scowled. He remembered the man from church. Emmett said this Pat no-good was the killer of his pa. Eric's legs felt weak and now, suddenly, it wasn't so exciting; it was horribly real and not particularly pleasant.

'No,' Pat said. 'My boss Mr Hart says to leave you in here. If we need you, we'll let you know.'

It seemed that Pat was to stay on guard here – the killer of the sheriff in the sheriff's office.

Eric slunk away to report back to the others in the livery.

Hart and Kendall rode out of town with two men. They halted at the town sign and Hart gestured at the roadside, opposite. 'This'll do, just here.'

The men dismounted and while one used a hammer to remove the warning about weapons, the other unfastened another sign from his horse. They nailed it to the post. It read:

NO ENTRY

TOWN CLOSED

CHOLERA

'That'll keep a lid on the place,' Hart said, 'and prevent out-lying farmers and ranchers from coming in, I reckon.'

'Sure is a good plan, Boss,' said Kendall. 'If anyone who comes this way can read, of course.'

Hart glared. 'It's going to be a tense time without any out-siders muddying the waters.' He eyed the man with a hammer. 'Put the other sign on the north bank of the creek, by the bridge entrance.'

'Sure, boss.'

As his two men rode back to town, Hart turned in his saddle and said, 'You're still finding objections, Heath. What gives?'

'You know me, Boss. I just want things straight in my mind.'

'Yeah, I know. We've been through a lot since . . . since we fought the war.'

'Well, Boss, it doesn't sit easy with me, you shooting a woman – whatever the reason.'

Hart swore then laughed out loud. 'Hell, I didn't intend to kill her – or anyone, for that matter. Just needed to shake 'em

48

up, scare the living hell out of 'em!'

'Just fortunate her husband was the doctor, I guess,' said Kendall.

'Yeah, it was, wasn't it?' Hart laughed again.

But Kendall didn't laugh.

CHAPTER 4

DEVIL'S ADVOCATE

Monday

In his crumpled grey suit and grubby white shirt, Simeon Gray stood on the walkway overlooking the hardpan at the entrance to the main mine. Clustered below were his miners, all of them fully clothed and relatively clean. A far cry from their appearance after several hours in the mine, while they worked in the only light afforded by candles and the odd oil-lamp, suffering the heat from the depths, most of them stripped down to breechcloths or long underwear bottoms cut at mid-thigh. Briefly, he explained to his miners what had happened.

A few miners grumbled.

Gray gripped the wooden rail, his knuckles whitening. 'If we don't continue to mine and process silver, they will kill a hostage.'

To emphasize the point, Emily stepped forward with Naomi, her gun raised to Naomi's head.

Naomi still wore the clothes she'd been apprehended in the day before: a pale green blouse with bell sleeves and a matching dark green linen skirt, belted at the waist.

'Begging your pardon, Mr Gray,' said one miner in the group, hands nervously scrunching his skullcap, 'but she's your daughter and has nothing to do with any of us.'

Naomi let out a shocked gasp. Emily chuckled coarsely.

Simeon Gray groaned, clenched his fists, and rested them on the wooden rail. 'I hadn't finished. It isn't only my Naomi's life at risk. They're holding hostages all over town and will kill one every hour if you don't work in the mine.'

A few men seemed abashed, looking down, scraping their heavy shoes in the dirt.

'So, what's in it for us?' asked Donnelly.

Hart stepped forward and aimed his pistol at Donnelly, cocked it. 'You get to live. Now, you've got ten miners – I suggest you get to work. You've wasted enough time as it is. They must all do what they're told. Or we start killing the women.'

Donnelly's face broke out in glistening sweat. He glanced round at the others.

'Brad says they've got the bordello under guard.'

'Bastards!'

'They've got my Janet,' said Sheldon McTavish, the chief of mining.

Grim-faced, Donnelly nodded. 'Let's go to work, men!'

Reluctantly, the miners followed him to the lower cave entrance.

'That's very sensible of them,' Hart said.

Emily lowered her gun and Simeon Gray sighed with relief. Naomi let out a slight moan, swayed and then held on to the wooden rail. Mrs McTavish ran to her aid, supported her.

Shots sounded, coming from the town hall. 'What's going on?' Hart demanded.

*

Carl Watzman, the town drunk, went undiscovered in the basement of a ramshackle townhouse diagonally opposite the town hall. When he opened his eyes and peered out of the window slit at ground level, he sobered up very quickly, hastily making an assessment of the situation. Armed men paced outside the town hall and, if he leaned forward and squinted, at the end of Mine Street he could see more sentries. All of them complete strangers. He suddenly didn't want to hang around this town any more.

Furtively, he climbed the basement stairs and reached the front door. He opened it just a crack. His hands trembled and he licked his lips, in dire need of a drink. Liquid sustenance would have to wait, he decided; now, he needed to rely on steady legs. He swung open the door and ran to the right, towards the bridge.

Hurting in his heart and chest, Emmett sat disconsolately on a barrel at the corner of Mr Ream's Municipal Bank; from here he could watch the town hall, the bridge and the mine entrance.

He immediately recognized Carl Watzman running with an awkward gait and was about to shout a warning, but he was too late.

One of the sentries at the bridge raised his rifle, fired and shot Watzman in the leg. Watzman collapsed in the dirt, groaning, clutching his bloody thigh.

The man ran up to Watzman and dragged him, crying and pleading for a drink, towards the town hall.

Emmett felt a chill skitter down his spine as Bret Pike stepped out on to the porch of the town hall. Pike grinned when he saw Watzman being dragged along, and then shouted in through the open door, 'Hey, bring the hostages, get them to watch at the windows!'

When Pike seemed sure that he had an audience, he drew his pistol. 'This is what happens if anyone tries to leave.' In the blink of an eye, he shot Watzman in the head, right there on the town hall steps.

Emmett's stomach lurched violently. Somehow, this seemed worse than the shooting of Pa. Mr Watzman was unarmed; he'd never seen anyone shot in cold blood like that. Then he felt the blood drain from his face as Bret Pike pointed his six-gun at him. 'And that goes for women and *children* as well!'

'You fiend!' Mayor Travis shouted from the doorway.

'Sticks and stones don't hurt.' Bret laughed and swerved round, aimed his gun at the mayor. 'Only lead hurts me; and we hold all the bullets in this town. Just watch how you shoot off at the mouth, Mayor, or I might just shoot it right off of you!'

Mrs Travis urged her husband back inside.

Bret gestured at the pair from the bridge sentry duty. 'Drag him away somewhere out of sight.'

'Where, Bret?'

'I don't care! Just where I don't have to smell his corpse.' He turned back to the doorway, then hesitated, faced them again. 'Dig a big hole in boot hill, put him in but don't cover it just yet.'

'Don't cover it?'

Bret Pike nodded. 'That's what I said. I wouldn't be surprised if we don't have a few more bodies to throw in there before we're finished!'

Emmett's heart pounded. He ground his teeth together and clenched his fists. He feared Bret Pike wasn't exaggerating.

As the two men grabbed an arm apiece, Hart and Emily strode hurriedly towards them along Mine Street. Hart hollered, 'What's all the shooting about?'

Bret holstered his gun and gestured at the corpse. 'Just shot him trying to sneak out of town.'

'OK.' Hart and Emily climbed the town hall steps. 'That should keep them all docile inside!'

The pair entered the foyer, Bret by their side.

The hostages lay in groups along the walls. A few were rising, stretching doubtless stiff limbs, and rubbing sleep from eyes, while the majority lay still, miserable, eyeing their captors.

Hart stopped in the middle of the floor and announced, 'I need to speak to the man who runs your bank!' He turned to Emily.

Emily pulled out a sheaf of papers, scanned them, and then bawled, 'Grafton Ream!'

'Thank you, my dear.' Hart eyed the group of hostages. 'So who's going to tell me where he is?'

'We sure ain't going to make it easy for you bastards to rob us,' snapped Shelly, glaring at Emily while she absently adjusted her dress.

Fawn-coloured eyes narrowed, Emily took a threatening step towards Shelly, her usually sensual lips twisted.

Just at that moment a fair-haired tall and wiry man pushed to the front of a group of women. He wore a light grey suit, waistcoat and vest. 'No need for that, young woman!' His chin was clean-shaven; his moustache joined his sideburns. He turned to Hart. 'I'm Grafton Ream, the president of the bank.'

Before Ream could react, Bret and Hart rushed him and a brief scuffle broke out.

While Bret held Ream, Hart pulled the derringer free from the banker's vest pocket. 'I'll have that, Mr Ream. Don't want any innocent bystanders getting hurt, do we?' Hart eyed Shelly meaningfully.

Catching his breath, Ream shrugged against Bret's tight grip. 'I suppose you're going to rob the bank as well?'

Hart signed to Bret to release his hold. 'Yes, I might make a withdrawal. But later, when we're about to leave.'

Massaging his freed arm, Ream said, 'Stealing all that silver – that's going to badly affect the town.'

'So? What do you care? You're a banker.'

'As a banker, I'm here to help the community, not for personal aggrandisement and gain.'

'Yeah, and pigs can fly!' snorted Bret.

Ream's facial hair seemed to bristle. 'Robbing their bank is going to destroy them. Many have entrusted me with their life savings.'

Hart's hand darted up to Ream's face and squeezed his pale cheeks. 'You won't make things awkward, now will you?' He let go.

'I'd be a fool to try, wouldn't I?'

'That's what I thought.' Hart grinned. 'But so you don't get any ideas, Bret here will be your constant companion. When I give the order, we take a stroll to the bank and you open the safe and help put the money in bags. Got it?'

Morosely, Ream nodded.

Satisfied everything was in control in the town hall, Hart returned to the mine office.

Theo Leese's face went red and he jumped in his seat as the telegraph starting clacking. Jesus, it was a while since he'd used the damned thing. He leaned over the desk, jotting down the rest of the message. When it ended, he breathed a sigh of relief. He hadn't missed much and no reply was needed.

He read his scribble, his lips moving with each word, and then he groaned. Mr Hart ain't going to like this, not one bit.

Scrunching the message sheet in his jeans pocket, he strode out of the telegraph office and half ran, half trotted towards the mine entrance.

55

He felt real important as the sentries let him in when he said he had a vital message.

He climbed the wooden stairs to the mine owner's office and knocked on the door.

'Who is it?' Hart's voice answered.

'It's me, sir, Theo. I've got a wire – an important message.'

The door swung open and Hart stood there, a cigar dangling from the corner of his mouth, his wide-set, steel-grey eyes glaring. 'Well, let me have it, man!'

Theo dug it out, straightened the sheet a little and handed it over.

Hart scanned it and growled, 'Shit!'

Kendall strode up behind him. 'What's the problem, Boss?'

'The circuit judge is due on Wednesday's stage – for the trial of Monty Blake.'

'So what?'

Hart turned, puffing on his cigar. 'The mysterious absence of a circuit judge might get noticed, that's what!'

'Yeah, I see what you mean. Can you tell him not to bother? Maybe say the prisoner's escaped – or died.'

Hart shook his head. 'Either reason would need an investigation. He'd come anyway.' He turned back to Theo. 'Send a reply: We'll be ready for the trial.'

Theo nodded, praying he could remember how to send a message.

'We will?' Kendall queried.

'No,' Hart snapped, 'of course we won't. But we've got to behave like everything's all normal.'

'You'll make a slip, be sure of it,' warned Simeon Gray. 'People are afraid of your gunmen; they won't act normal.'

Hart swung round, slapping the back of his hand against Gray's cheek. 'Normal is what I say it is!'

Gray rubbed his reddened face, his eyes darting in anger.

He pursed his lips.

'Speaking of normal routine,' Hart added, 'when is the next shipment of silver scheduled to leave?'

'Friday. We transport out every Friday. I wire Wells, Fargo for an armed escort.'

Hart nodded. 'You'll do that, as if everything's normal. How many in the escort?'

'Four.'

'We can handle four.' Hart turned to Kendall. 'We'll take care of the escort when they get here.'

'Sure, Boss,' Kendall said. 'But won't Wells, Fargo wonder about their men?'

'Yes. . . ' He looked askance at Kendall. 'You seem to be raising a lot of objections, lately.'

Kendall shrugged. 'Just being Devil's advocate, Boss.'

'OK . . . you're right, I hadn't figured on this escort business. Maybe we'll cut short our stay here – leave on Saturday. Before they miss the Wells, Fargo men.'

'What are you doing, Emmett?' his ma called up from the parlour.

He stopped, standing precariously on tiptoes on a chair as he reached up to the top of the bedroom wardrobe. 'Just tidying up my room, Ma!'

She laughed briefly. 'Will wonders never cease? If your pa could see. . . .' Then she gulped and sobbed.

An aching emptiness filled Emmett and he squashed it down with burning hatred. He gritted his teeth. 'I won't be long, Ma.' He reached a little further then his fingertips touched the tin. He carefully clutched it and drew it to his chest then stepped off the chair.

He opened the lid and poured the coins on to his bed – his savings from chores, money he'd been putting aside towards a rifle. He put some in each pants pocket then rushed to the window. He glanced briefly towards the dresser, where he'd left a hastily scrawled note to his mother: *Gone to stay with Gene. Love, Emmett.*

Well, it wasn't a complete lie, he thought as he clambered out of the window and ran over to Gene, who was waiting in the shadows.

'Have you got your savings?' Emmett asked.

'Yeah,' Gene whispered. 'But what do we need the money for?'

Emmett glanced over his shoulder at the open window of his bedroom. 'Let's get away from here first.'

They ran past the row of houses that skirted Rabbit Creek, clinging to shadows as they went. At the corner, they stopped and Gene checked it was clear before they turned into East Street and stopped. They easily ducked under the fence behind the fruit and vegetable store and rushed across the tilled back yard filled with kitchen herbs. Slinking under the fence, they entered the livery. Here, they met with Alice, Maura and Eric.

Alice said, 'Those two sentries are still down there, by the creek.'

'At the palisade end?'

'Yes. They just stand and smoke.'

'OK.' Emmett sank to his knees on the straw-covered floor. He pulled out a big handkerchief and poured his chore money on to it. 'Gene, tip yours in, come on.'

A little reluctantly, Gene fished in his pants pocket and added his coins to the small pile.

Sombrely, Alice, Maura and Eric added their savings – nickels and dimes.

Alice knelt beside him and said, 'What's this all about, Emmett?'

Rage burned inside him. He pursed his lips, determined. 'None of our townspeople have got a gun now. Eric told us, he saw them all piled up in . . . in Pa's office. They can't fight back.'

'So?' Alice eyed the pile of coins.

Emmett tied the corners of the handkerchief together and hefted the weighty bundle. 'We've gotta get outside help, and this'll pay for it.'

Maura made a scoffing sound. 'You won't get much help for that!' She turned to Alice. 'How much is there, do you reckon?'

'Twenty-two dollars and forty cents.'

Gene stared, agog.

'Boys!' Alice rolled her eyes to the heavens. 'I can add up in my head.'

'It's a down payment,' Emmett said hastily.

'Maybe so,' Eric said, 'but where do we go for help?'

'Yeah,' said Gene.

All eyes were on Emmett now as he shoved the small bundle of coins into his pocket.

Silence reigned briefly.

'Well?' urged Alice.

'The nearest town is Mesita. I have an idea who might help when we get there.'

Maura stood up, dusted off some straw from her dress. 'That's a long way for us to walk.'

'We all can't go,' Emmet said. 'I reckon we'd stand a better chance if only Gene and I went.'

Gene swallowed. 'Just us?'

'You left a note, like I told you, didn't you?'

'Oh, heck, I forgot!'

Emmett turned to Alice. 'Write a note for him and give it to his pa – when we've gone.'

She nodded. Her eyes were wide, glistening.

'We'll meet up in the livery.' He thumbed his chin, calculating, guessing, a mannerism he'd picked up from his pa. His next words came out thick, throaty, for some reason: 'Sometime Tuesday.'

Alice shook her head. 'Sometime Tuesday isn't good enough, Emmett, and you know it!'

'Sundown Tuesday, then. Or dawn Wednesday. Hell, I really don't know for sure.'

'There's no need to use that kind of language,' Alice berated. Then she nodded. 'All right. I think we can explain our absence so we can meet you here at that time.'

Impulsively, she leaned forward and kissed him on his cheek. 'Take care, both of you.'

He felt his face flush and noticed that Gene leaned forward expectantly for a kiss but didn't receive one. Inside his chest, he glowed warm, just a little.

That Monday evening, they started loading the first wagon with silver ingots. Hart supervised, gazing down from the manager's balcony. Over to the right were three more wagons they'd commandeered.

At first, he'd thought of sending the wagons out when they were full, straight to the railhead, to be met by Tom, his brother. But that was a big risk. Best to stockpile all wagons here and take them out together when they left the town for good on Saturday. Both Calhoun and Grant liked that idea, too.

Mrs Dent was kept busy providing pies, potatoes and beans. The first meal delivery on the buckboard was to the man in the telegraph office, and then on to the town hall. She climbed the steps with her weighty tray of pies, but none of the gang offered to help.

It fleetingly crossed her mind to put rat poison in the pies, but she had no way of targeting just the gang. Her heart lurched as she saw Mr Ream sitting so despondent with the mayor. They looked helpless. She fleetingly smiled at them and even at the girl Shelly from the bordello. Despite her calling, the girl had been brave to stand up to that Hart fellow.

Mrs Dent felt a little guilty, being free, not a hostage. Thank God her Larry wasn't a hostage, either – the gang couldn't do without food or the livery to look after their horses.

As she laid the food on the long table in the meeting hall, she murmured, 'I hope I'll get recompense for all this food – I need to replace my supplies, you know.'

The gang leader, Hart, chuckled. 'You'll get paid, don't worry. Maybe in silver ingots!'

'I don't want payment with stolen silver!'

'Too bad – that's all we've got.' He leaned close, threatening. 'If you don't provide for my men and our hostages, we'll find someone else who will, and you can join them in the jail, behind bars.'

She nodded, deciding she wasn't cut out to be brave like that Shelly girl. She cocked her head to one side as she noticed there was a queue at the rear of the room.

Hart chuckled. 'There's always a queue for the outhouse, ma'am – I'm sure it don't reflect on your cookin'.'

Her cheeks reddened. She flounced out and clambered up on to the buckboard seat.

Next stop, the mine compound. The sentry at the gate seemed a mite jumpy, even though by now he should be used to her regular visits with food. If he didn't like it, maybe he should have chosen a different profession. The sentries relieved her of the food at the gate, which suited her fine.

After she'd done that, she parked the vehicle outside the jail.

Before entering, she glanced down the street. But she

couldn't see The Passion Flower from here. She'd been told Miss Larkin was taking care of the food for those at her premises. Probably more superior fare than meat pies, potatoes and beans, she thought begrudgingly. Wages of sin paid better, she reckoned.

The man who shot Sheriff Rosco stepped out of the office. 'Took your time. I'm starving!'

She shrugged and stepped down with the box of food for the prisoners. 'I'll give them their food first, if you don't mind.' She strode past him and abruptly she tripped over his extended leg. She stumbled forward as he laughed uproariously. She couldn't balance with the food box in front of her and clattered to her knees. The box burst open and the food spilled all over the floor.

'Next time, don't give me any sass, you hear?' He gestured at the open door to the jail section. 'Scrape up what you can and they can have that – or do without.'

Her knees felt bruised and her pride was even more damaged. Blinking back tears, she reached for a couple of plates, the mash and beans half on them, half on the floor.

Pat growled, 'I said clean up – after you've fed me!' He swore. 'This town's a dead loss when it comes to feeding me, it seems!'

Mrs Dent paled at the reference to that fateful Sunday – a mere two days gone. Her vision blurred as tears fell for the sheriff, his wife and son.

Visibility was quite good, Emmett reckoned. The moon was bright; in two more nights it would be full. He'd been out hunting with Gene on many a moonlit evening and was used to creeping through the undergrowth after rabbits and the odd raccoon. They easily avoided the two sentries, who seemed more interested in chatting and smoking than being alert, and waded into Rabbit Creek. The water wasn't particularly cold and the muddy bottom had enough embedded stones to provide purchase. The bundle of coins tended to weigh Emmett down a little on one side but he persevered and, stiff-legged, hauled himself forward.

A few minutes later, dripping wet, they heaved themselves out through a cluster of reeds. Bullfrogs croaked.

Standing well hidden in the reeds, Emmett removed his coin bundle then took off his clothes, wrung them out. 'Wet, they'll slow us down,' he said.

Nodding, Gene stripped, too.

Emmett studied the stars and moved at a slight angle from the creek. 'We head southeast, we'll get on the Mesita trail.'

'If you say so.' Gene's tone sounded as if he was unconvinced.

Seconds later, Emmett sank up to his waist in a noisome marsh. He swore and then said, 'Sorry, Ma.'

'She ain't here, she won't know.'

'Oh, yeah.' He waded through the foul-smelling water, each movement seeming to generate pungent sulphurous smells. 'We're going to get slowed down in this,' he said.

Gene gasped. 'What was that?' He pointed.

Emmett chuckled. 'Just a will o' wisp. . . .'

'I – I read about them, they're evil spirits. Let's go back, try another way.'

'No, we can't. We'd leave an easy wet muddy trail for the sentries to follow as soon as we got out the creek.'

'Why do you think of everything?'

Emmett chuckled. 'I read books, that's why.'

'Oh, yeah, how could I forget?'

CHAPTER 5

'YOU'RE ALL HEROES'

Tuesday

The swamp ended as it trickled into the rugged boulders at the base of the narrow Parnham Gorge that split the land for about a mile. The moonlight barely penetrated into this cleft, but somehow, the boys managed to clamber up the southern side of the gorge. From now on, the land should be dry.

Emmett shivered, hoping that dawn wouldn't be too far off.

Finally, sunrise offered welcoming warmth. Exhausted, shivering, Emmett supported Gene with an arm round his friend's shoulders.

They'd been walking all night and now Emmett was having difficulty seeing straight. He kept shutting his eyes, and each time woke with a start as Gene knocked against him and they both almost tumbled to the ground.

If they didn't get to Mesita and shelter soon, Emmett reckoned they'd be done for. It seemed absurd to be so thirsty, considering they'd been soaked to the skin until only a few

64

miles back; since then, their clothes had dried out. Maybe that was why he shivered? The wet clothes had robbed him of his body heat.

He couldn't go on another step. Abruptly, he stopped and lowered Gene to the ground.

Gene let out a croak but nothing more and curled up where he lay.

Emmett rubbed his eyes. His heart thudded in his chest. The peak of the big top was visible above the heat haze, he felt sure. Though he wasn't totally convinced; he'd read about mirages. 'The circus, Gene, we're almost there!' But the words barely passed his lips, he was so weak.

Despite the need to investigate that distant tent pinnacle, he sat on the hard earth and grinned, tears tingling through the grime on his cheeks. 'We've made it!' he whispered.

'What?' Gene said dozily.

'Nothing.' He lay down beside Gene and closed his eyes.

The trumpeting of an elephant roused him.

Startled, aching in his legs and back, Emmett glanced at the sky. The sun was directly overhead. Mid-morning. He'd slept longer than he'd expected. Precious time wasted! Frantically, he shook Gene. 'Come on, wake up, we've got to go!'

Dazedly, Gene got to his feet, wiping sleep from his eyes.

Hayley Rosco woke. Half the bed was empty. And it would always be so. . . . She hardly recalled what she'd done after the funeral on Sunday. God almighty, that was over a day ago.

She got up and went into Emmett's bedroom, realizing that he must be hurting, too, though she confessed to herself that she was really seeking his company.

She saw the note immediately. But that was yesterday. Would he stay overnight? She felt guilt, not looking after him. She felt awful, allowing her grief to overpower her. She must do better.

She returned to her bedroom and washed at the basin, then dressed.

Her stomach rumbled emptily, but she had no appetite for breakfast. She hurried round to North Street, where there was a staircase behind the Rabbit's Hole Saloon. At the top of the stairs, she hesitated, her heart hammering, and then, steeling herself, she knocked on the door.

Alden Tubbs answered; she'd never got used to his glass eye, it was still quite unnerving. His pot belly showed considerably since he was only in his long johns and boots, quite unabashed. He scratched his rat's nest beard. 'I guess you've come about this?' he said and held out a scrap of paper. 'Gene says he's with your Emmett.' He had a throaty voice. 'Has he been misbehaving?'

She suddenly felt faint and supported herself against the doorjamb. If her stomach hadn't been empty, she might have retched.

'Are you all right, Mrs Rosco?' With surprising gentleness for a big-boned man, he took hold of her arms. 'Do you want to come in and sit down?'

She shook her head. 'Oh, dear Lord,' she moaned, 'what are they up to now?'

'Up to?' Alden looked puzzled and concerned now, and scratched his grizzled hair. 'What do you mean?'

'Gene didn't stay with us, Mr Tubbs.' Her hand trembling, she showed him Emmett's note.

'Why, the lyin'—'

At that moment, Alice called up from the foot of the staircase, 'Excuse me, are you looking for Emmett and Gene?'

Alice climbed the stairs and moved inside.

Hayley and Alden followed and he shut the door.

Without being invited, Alice sat in a chair, her hands in her lap. 'Both your sons are quite safe. They've gone for help.'

Hayley felt faint all over again and Alden guided her to a sofa, where she sat heavily. 'First, Tad . . . now Emmett. Oh, God!'

'Take it easy, Mrs Rosco,' Alden whispered, 'I'm sure Emmett's all right. We'll soon get to the bottom of this.' He eyed Alice severely and demanded, 'What kind of help?' He scratched his beard. 'They're only kids! What can they do?'

Emmett and Gene's bodies were blessed with the wondrous recuperative powers of the young. Their aches and pains seemed to fizzle away as they absorbed the smells, sounds and colours of the circus environment. With renewed vigour, they sneaked into the grounds and crawled under the edge of the big tent.

Emmett grinned. This was the final procession round the ring. The entire audience was applauding. 'Now they're finished, Gene, they can help us!'

Gene stared. 'The circus people? Why'd they want to do that? I thought you were getting help from the sheriff of Mesita – and maybe a posse.'

'Nope.' Emmett shook his head. 'Mesita's sheriff's an old man – and the town's well known for keeping to itself. I thought you knew that.'

'Well, no, I didn't. And you sure didn't get that from no book.'

'No, I overheard the barber telling Pa. . . .' He stopped as it hit home that he would never see Pa again or hear his gossip.

'Hey, you two!' shouted a brawny man wielding a cudgel. 'You haven't paid!'

'Come on, let's scoot!' Emmett urged and pulled up the tent edge. Gene darted under and he followed.

Seconds later, big hands grasped the collars of both Gene and Emmett and suddenly they were both suspended in the air.

Emmett suddenly had difficulty breathing. His collar was too tight round his neck. Through teary eyes he noticed that Gene looked in a bad way as well.

'Diego, tell your brutes to let them down!'

It was a woman who spoke, Emmett reckoned, and she had a warm, caring voice. He blacked out.

Josefa smiled down at the two boys where they sat on the edge of a narrow bed of furs in the capacious wagon, sipping mugs of coffee. Standing at the entrance flap, Mateo studied them also, stroking his pointed beard. Diego sat opposite them on another bed.

She laid a hand on the shoulder of the freckled lad. 'Didn't I see you in Conejos Blancos?'

Lowering his coffee mug, the boy said, 'Yes, ma'am. Name's Emmett, Emmett Rosco—'

'The sheriff's son,' she said. 'Yes, now I remember.'

'I'm Gene, his best friend.'

Josefa studied them both, surprised at their appearance.

Diego growled, 'Don't you know you could be in deep trouble, sneaking in without paying?'

Looking glum, the pair nodded.

'Leave them be, Diego, they're doing no harm,' Josefa said. 'The show's over.'

'That may be so, but I've a good mind to send these two back to the sheriff. His father will know how to chastise him.'

Emmett's lips quivered. Something was wrong; Josefa felt it in her bones.

Gene stood and moved protectively in front of Emmett, his face screwed-up. 'Leave him be! His pa's dead – murdered on Sunday!'

'Oh, *Madre de Dios.*' Josefa's heart somersaulted and she knelt in front of Emmett. She grasped his shoulders gently. 'Is this so?'

Tears rimmed his eyes as he nodded. 'Yes . . . . We escaped to get help – your help,' he croaked.

'Escaped?' Diego echoed.

'The town's been taken over by a bunch of *desperados*,' Emmett said in a quavering voice.

'And they're going to rob the mine!' Gene added. 'We've been walking all night!'

Josefa eyed Mateo. 'That explains the state they're in.' She gestured at their muddy clothes, dirty faces and tired eyes.

Emmett shrugged off her concern. 'It doesn't matter about us, ma'am. They've taken everybody's guns.' Then, haltingly, he explained how the town had been so swiftly taken over, mentioning the wounding of the doctor's wife and the murder of the town drunk, Mr Watzman. Between them they enumerated the number of sentries and guards they'd spotted – sixteen plus five leaders. 'We need your help, ma'am.' He delved into his pants pockets and brought out a weighty handkerchief bundle, opened it and displayed many coins. He held them out to her. 'We can pay.'

'Yes,' said Gene. He looked at Emmett, seemingly at a loss to say more.

Emmett said, as though his words were rehearsed, 'You're all heroes. We've seen how good you are with so many weapons. And I – we – reckon you could whup the bad guys real good.'

Gene nodded vigorously. 'Yeah, you're handy with knives, guns and bow and arrows – sure, you could—'

Diego held up a hand. 'Wait, that's enough!' He sighed, adjusted his tight-fitting vest. 'I sympathize with your town's plight.' He pursed his lips. 'And I'm sorry about the sheriff – I mean, your father – but I have a business to run.' He was about to say more, it seemed, but stopped and stared at Josefa as she spoke.

'Mateo, get the family together,' she said.

Diego shook his head, his jowls wobbling. 'No, Josefa, you can't be serious about this.'

She offered him one of her smiles. 'We're just going to discuss it.'

A few minutes later, the rest of the Mendoza troupe crowded into the wagon.

Ramón said, 'Mateo's told us everything.'

Antonio eyed Emmett. 'Is Naomi – I mean, Miss Gray – is she all right, son?'

Emmett evaded his piercing, deep brown eyes. 'I don't know for sure, Mr Rivera, but I think so. She's being held prisoner in the mine office with her pa.'

Josefa had never seen Antonio look so tense, so angry. He'd never seemed to care a fig for any woman before; he simply used them. But something now in his manner was different. Maybe he was a changed man.

'I must go,' Antonio said, casting his gaze on the others. The look was plain enough: come with me.

Diego grunted in disgust. 'How can you agree to help those gringos?' he demanded.

José nodded. 'We owe that town nothing!'

'They beat up Ignacio,' Juan argued.

Arcadia clung to Juan's arm. 'And our takings weren't so hot, either.'

'It wasn't the whole town who attacked Ignacio,' Josefa said, 'just a couple of drunk miners.'

'Josefa has a point,' Ramón said, his tone reasonable. 'We shouldn't brand all gringos the same.'

'Why not?' snapped José. 'They do exactly that to us!'

Arms akimbo, Juan said, 'José is right. Why put ourselves in danger for gringos?'

'Precisely!' Diego shouted.

'Then I will go alone!' snapped Antonio.

'No, you won't,' Josefa said. 'I'll go with you.' She glanced at José and gleaned pleasure from his disapproval, his face twisting.

'Where my wife goes, so must I,' said Mateo, resting an arm on her shoulders.

'This is ridiculous!' José barked, glaring at Josefa.

'You forget,' Diego said, 'you're going up against desperate men – killers. You heard the boy; they've murdered two people, shot a woman. When was the last time any of you fired a weapon in anger or killed anyone?'

Ramón cleared his throat, pushed out his chest. 'We've done our fair share of fighting, Diego – before we joined your circus. None of us might like it, but we've spilled blood in our defence and that of our loved ones.'

'This is different!' Diego snapped.

Mateo shrugged and stroked his moustache, studying Juan, Arcadia and José. 'I recall my cousin telling me about seven gringos who helped his *pueblo* against many *bandidos*.'

Juan laughed. 'That was just a story.'

'No, it was true.' Mateo pulled a gleaming knife from the sash round his waist. 'Pepe showed me his bullet wound scars,' He gently touched the blade point to his left arm, the bicep and the forearm. 'Here and here.' He jabbed his chest, below the heart. 'And here. . . . He was lucky to survive. Not all of the gringos survived.'

'Precisely,' Diego said again. 'You would risk your life and the lives of your family – your entire troupe – for strangers?'

'The two little gringos have offered us much.'

Diego guffawed. 'Twenty dollars?'

'Twenty-two and forty cents!' Gene corrected.

Smiling, Mateo returned the knife to his sash. 'No, Diego, I do not speak of the money they have offered. It's called faith. These

71

boys have faith in us, my friend.' He scanned the rest of them and one by one they nodded agreement. 'Just so.' Mateo smiled. 'You go on, Diego. We will catch you up in Colorado Springs.'

'This is utter foolishness.' Diego shook his head and made his way to the exit flap. 'You're all crazy, but I will pray for you.'

Josefa smiled at the circus owner. He clearly wanted to be angry, but he couldn't bring himself to be, and she understood this as she looked at the trusting faces of the two boys, Emmett and Gene. They'd melted all their hearts, she felt sure.

'But I don't know what I will do to replace the Magnificent Mendozas!' Then Diego flung the flap aside and left.

Emmett stood up. 'Ma'am, I thought all of the circus people would come back to help.'

Mateo chuckled. 'Sorry, young man, but your rate of pay is not very enticing. You get seven of us – the Magnificent Mendozas. That should be enough.'

Eyes and mouth wide, Gene stared, then said, 'Seven against twenty-one?'

Mateo nodded. 'Three-to-one – not bad odds, I think. Your Texas Rangers would be comfortable with these odds, no? Besides, we will have the element of surprise.'

Tuesday in town was eventful, which surprised Hart. He'd noticed how most of the townsfolk went about their daily business as if they were walking on eggshells. As Gray had admitted, they couldn't pretend life was normal.

They'd already had one minor shooting and two fist-fights with the locals.

He really worried what it would be like by Saturday. Keeping a lid on the men till then was going to be hard. Frayed tempers were already riding high. Just as well he'd decided to cut short their occupation of the town; they'd never have coped with two weeks.

Confiscating all the guns was a smart move, sure enough. So far, the doctor was kept busy fixing bruises and a few broken bones, and a bullet wound in an arm and a knife wound in someone else's leg. He hoped that was all the medic would have to contend with.

Hayley Rosco sat with Alden Tubbs in the Rabbit's Hole Saloon, both nursing glasses of untouched whiskey. 'I can't be a good mother,' she moaned. 'I wasn't there for him when – when Tad—'

'That's not so, Hayley. But I feel the same way. I can't hold down this saloon and be a proper father as well. Kids need two parents these days. There's too many distractions for them, I reckon. In my day, we only knew work, chores aplenty – never had much time to run off and play.'

She reached across the table, rested her hand on his. 'Maybe we could help each other – when the boys get back?'

'Hey, lady,' a man said, resting a hand on her shoulder, making her start, 'I reckon you should be favouring me, not the barkeep. He can get his fun with you any time, but I need some tender loving care right now.'

She jerked round in her chair, shoved his hand off her.

The man grinned, doffed his hat. 'Name's Vince, missy.' His crooked teeth were yellow and he was in need of a shave, and his shirt was stained with sweat. 'How about keeping me company upstairs?'

Alden scraped his chair back and stood. 'Have a care, mister. This lady—'

Vince sneered. 'She ain't no lady if she's in your saloon!'

Hayley leaned across the table, touched Alden's arm. 'Please, don't.' She turned to Vince. 'There's been a misunderstanding. I don't work here. And now, please step aside, I'm leaving!'

Vince grabbed her arm, crushed her to him; he smelled quite rank, made her feel faint. 'I don't think so, honey.' With his free hand, he flung a couple of coins on the table; they clattered to the floorboards. 'That'll pay.'

Suddenly, he glared sightlessly, let go of Hayley and crumpled to the floor.

Shaken, Hayley turned to see Kendall standing there, holding his six-gun butt first. 'Sorry about that, Mrs Rosco. Vince didn't realize who you were. He'll have a headache when he comes to – and serves him right.'

She glared, unable to formulate any words of thanks. Giving Alden a hasty nod, she swung on her heel and left.

While the Mendoza troupe had three wagons, they agreed with Diego only to take one, a covered wagon, and a horse for each of the seven – Mateo, Josefa, Antonio, Juan, Arcadia, José and Ramón.

Josefa noted that José was reluctant; she reasoned that the lovesick fool tagged along because he went where she went.

Sitting inside the wagon, Mateo said to Emmett, 'We need to know how this man Hart has deployed his men. Tell us while we travel.'

Emmett nodded. 'We have three spies – Alice, Maura and Eric – who can help, too.'

'And how old are they?' Josefa asked.

'Same as us,' Gene said. 'Why?'

'Just wondered.'

Emmett and Gene began to provide detailed information about the whereabouts of each sentry and guard as the wagon trundled through the moonlit night.

Riding alongside Antonio, Juan said, 'We need to free the hostages first, no?'

Antonio nodded. 'Easier said than done.' His mouth twisted.

'You think of Naomi, the mine owner's daughter?'

'Yes. The boy Gene, he saw them take her to the mine with her father.'

Juan nodded. 'It figures. Mr Gray knows the miners, the routines, doesn't he?'

Antonio swore.

Juan shook his head. 'I don't think Mateo has thought this through properly.'

'Why?'

'How are we to stop from killing them? If they start shooting, we'll have no option but to fight back – and to kill.'

'Juan, he's trying to do the right thing. If we kill some of Hart's men, then we could end up in a bloodbath.'

Juan shrugged. 'So?'

'So I don't want anything to happen to Naomi. Is that so difficult to understand?'

'She's a gringo mine owner's daughter. You are not a suitable match for her, I assure you.'

Antonio swore again and urged his horse forward, away from Juan.

Using his black cane with its silver handle, Virgil Perry tapped it on the floor as he walked into the guest lounge of the Talbot Hotel.

'One customer for you, Virgil,' said Doc. 'I'll patch up the other one.'

'Fine, very fine,' said Virgil. Inwardly, he smiled, not his normal reaction when faced with a cadaver. But this was different. One of the leaders, Calhoun, lay dead on the floor, a knife protruding from his chest. Cards lay scattered about. The one called Kendall stood by the body, as if guarding it. Over on a chair, another man whimpered while gripping his right arm, a deep knife slash bleeding copiously. Doc Ulrich knelt beside him, said, 'Let's take a look – doesn't seem so bad.'

'What do you know?'

'That's enough lip, Grant,' snapped Kendall. 'The doc's here to help. Shut it!'

Grant scowled. 'But it hurts like hell!'

'Don't be an ungrateful bastard,' Kendall growled, and strode away.

Ungrateful bastard, Virgil thought; that's true enough. Two of them out of action, he thought grimly. Now, if only they'd continue to fight among themselves. . . .

He shook his head and wondered how many more would succumb before the town returned to normal. He used his cane to measure the corpse. Good riddance.

While the two boys slept, exhausted, Josefa sat with Mateo as he drove the wagon. 'We can't free all the hostages at the same time, surely?' she said.

Mateo puffed on his cigar. 'We have to – otherwise, the alarm could go up and they might make good their threat. I don't want the blood of hostages on my hands.'

'It's Hart's men who'll have blood on their hands, not us,' she promised.

'It's the blood of innocents, all the same.'

Riding alongside the wagon, José said, 'Diego was right. This is madness. Even with the entire circus, we'd still be outgunned and outclassed.'

Mateo laughed round his cigar. 'Outgunned, maybe. Outclassed? I don't think so.' He grinned. 'Besides, we have weapons other than guns.' He winked at Josefa.

CHAPTER 6

'IT'S WHAT I DO'

Wednesday

'Stage is coming in!' bawled one of the guards, pointing at the slight slope that led to the bridge. Bret unfolded himself from the steps of the town hall and watched as the stagecoach crossed the bridge, noisily racketing over the wooden boards. It turned right, heading along Mine Street and passed the town hall in a flurry of dust. Bret squinted, his eyes suddenly grainy, and glimpsed two passengers. He ducked inside, called for Mansfield Akins. 'Hurry up, man! I need you to go to the mine, tell the boss we've got company!'

While Akins hurried off, Bret stepped down and walked diagonally across the wide expanse of the junction.

The stagecoach had pulled in outside the telegraph office, which also doubled as the stage depot. Theo Leese stood in the doorway.

The shotgun rider stepped down first, and said, 'You new around here?'

'Yeah,' Theo answered, eyes searching for someone or something.

'Thought so. Name's O'Leary.'

Bret stepped up. 'You sure don't look Irish, Mr O'Leary.'

'My pa was Mexican,' the shotgun rider said, opening the coach door and lowering the metal steps.

'Who – who've you got in there?' Theo asked.

'Circuit judge and a fine lady.' He helped the woman out first. She wore a hip-clinging red linen skirt, a broad black leather belt, a white silk blouse and black leather boots.

As the judge stepped down, Pat approached along the boardwalk. He wore a sheriff's star. 'I expect the judge would like to see the man he's trying, eh?'

'Sheriff Rosco?' the judge queried, extending his hand. 'I'm Judge Park.'

'Pat Hill.' Shaking hands, Pat added, 'Sorry, Sheriff Rosco's been called away . . . I've taken his place for the next few weeks. Pleased to meet you, Judge Park.'

'I was two minds whether to turn back or not,' the judge said.

'Why's that, sir?'

'The cholera notice.'

'Oh, yes, right. The doctor reckons he has it under control, but he wants the notice kept there just in case, you know?'

'Prudent, I suppose. Keeping a lid on it, yes, very prudent.'

'Yeah, a lid on it, that's right.'

'Where'd you want your trunk, Judge?' the stage driver called down.

Before the judge could answer, Pat said, 'Leave it in the depot for now. I'd like to show the judge the accused first. Then we'll get him all settled in.'

'OK.' The driver gestured to Theo. 'Give me a hand, will you? It's kinda heavy. I guess it's the judge's law books – weighty reading, eh?'

'Sure.' Theo stepped up and the pair manhandled the big

trunk to the boardwalk.

Pat turned to the woman passenger. 'Sorry, ma'am, it's mighty rude of me.' He doffed his hat briefly. 'If you'd care to come with me and the judge, I'll show you both to McGee's – the better of the two hotels in town.'

She curtseyed slightly. 'Thank you, Sheriff.'

'This way.' Pat led them past the lawyer's office and turned right into the jail. 'I have a little business to transact. If you wouldn't mind coming in for a moment, ma'am?'

'Certainly, Sheriff.'

They all stepped inside.

Then Pat drew his six-gun and levelled it on the judge and the woman. 'Our cells are getting kinda full, but I'm sure we can squeeze you two in.'

'What!' the woman shrieked.

Pat slammed his pistol against the side of her head and she stumbled into the judge.

The judge growled, 'What's the meaning of—?'

'Be quiet, the pair of you!' he whispered harshly. 'We want those stage men to leave here thinking nothing's wrong.'

'Wrong, sir?' the judge said. 'Hitting a defenceless woman like that is very wrong!'

'That's nothing to the wrong I can do, Judge. If you're quiet, I might let you live.' Pat scowled in thought, eyeing the judge. 'You ain't one of them hanging judges, are you?'

The judge's eyes narrowed and he pursed his lips.

'OK. Quiet is nice.' Pat kept his pistol on the two shaken passengers.

Then the office door opened and Hart walked in with Kendall by his side.

Kendall stuck his thumbs in his vest pockets and studied the woman. 'Don't damage her too much, Pat. She's got good looks – part Mex, part Indio, I reckon. Yeah, nice cheekbones.'

'I wasn't looking at her cheekbones.' Pat gave a dirty laugh. 'She was about to shout the place down. I needed to quieten her pronto.' He grinned. 'I reckon she's the sort who'll enjoy me getting a bit rough with her.'

'If Emily wasn't the jealous sort,' Hart said, 'I'd be tempted myself.' He gestured at Monty Blake who sat forlornly in a separate cell. 'OK, Blake, you come out and join us now. We need your cell.'

Pat sidled over to the sheriff's desk, retrieved the keys and opened Monty Blake's cell door.

Grabbing his hat and tucking his shirt in his waistband, Blake snagged a gun-belt, Colt and holster from the rack on the wall. 'Thanks, I'll be forever in your debt.' He licked his lips and hurried out.

Hart said, 'Inside, ma'am, Judge.'

'And be quick about it!' snapped Pat.

When the cell door was locked, Pat lowered himself into the chair and rested his feet up on the desk. 'Don't they look cosy? Did you have a word with the coach men?'

'Yeah,' Hart said, 'they're heading back to Alamosa in a couple of hours. Getting some shut-eye in the livery.'

Kendall frowned. 'No risk they'll talk to someone, that Dent guy, get word out?'

Hart shook his head. 'No. I've detailed a man – Tully – to go with them.'

Pat thumbed towards the cells. 'Why can't we just hold them as well?'

'They and their precious coach would be missed,' Kendall explained.

Hart studied the judge, who was administering to the woman's cut temple. 'I'll send a cable to Alamosa in the judge's name, explaining he's been called away to another case in Mogote.'

'Sounds good, Boss,' Kendall said.

Hart grinned. 'Looks like we've just got ourselves another important hostage!'

Pat eyed the woman. 'Two.'

Theo finished receiving a message for the lawyer next door and then acknowledged it. Yeah, it was all coming back to him, he thought as he spiked the sheet. Nothing important, just some answer to a legal inquiry, which didn't require a response.

He swung round on the chair and raised his feet to the desk. He knew he'd soon get bored – that's why he never stuck with the job after initial training and a couple of weeks in the office. A life of crime was much better. He chuckled. Though right now he was in a boring telegraph office. Go figure!

He heard a faint sound at the other end of the room. It came from beyond the curtain, near the luggage maybe. Mouse or rat, probably.

He swung his legs down and strode over to the curtain, a hand hovering over his handgun.

He drew the curtain back and stared into the blade of a knife.

'Don't make a sound, *señor*, and no harm will come to you.' The man was short, about five-two, with pale skin, his hair close-cropped. He wore a black and white leotard that revealed a sinewy physique with no fat. Around the man's waist a belt held three sheaths, and bolas.

Theo nodded.

'Good. My name is Ramón. What's yours?'

'Theo,' he squeaked.

'Right, Theo, let us, you and me, go to the telegraph desk and send a message.'

Theo nodded, then turned slowly and shuffled back to his chair and sat.

'Keep your hands where I can see them,' Ramón said, the

prick of the knife point against Theo's throat emphasizing the words.

Slowly, Theo reached out to the telegraph key.

'That is good, Theo. Send the following message to Fort Lyon.'

Theo jerked his head round and squealed as the point of the blade dug in.

'Just do as I ask.'

'Yes, Ramón.'

'*Bien.* Message reads: "Desperados have taken over our town. Conejos Blancos. Killed the sheriff. Town's people held hostage by twenty-one men. Bring immediate help."'

Theo hesitated at mention of the number of Hart's men, but quickly recovered and sent the full message.

Ramón eased the knife away, just a little, then sat on the edge of the desk. 'Now we wait for an answer.'

Theo rubbed his neck, brought his hand away, but there was no blood.

'I only cut when I mean to, Theo.'

Nodding, Theo said, 'How'd you get in here?' He thumbed at the bell over the door. 'I never saw or heard you enter.'

Ramón smiled. 'You helped carry me in.'

'Eh?' Then it dawned on him and he gasped. 'You were in the judge's trunk?'

'Yes, I was.' Ramón bowed his head only slightly, never taking his eyes from Theo. 'Ramón Mendoza, escapologist.'

Earlier in the day, not long after dawn, the Mendoza troupe had had a stroke of luck. Their wagon had crossed the trail of the inbound stagecoach. Sitting beside the shapely Josefa, Mateo accosted the driver and the stage pulled in.

There was only one passenger, the judge, and he introduced himself.

82

Once Mateo had explained about the town's predicament, the driver, the shotgun rider and Judge Park agreed to Mateo's hastily devised plan.

José and Antonio exchanged clothes with the driver and shotgun rider. José didn't need the driver's weapon as his holster held a Merwin Hulbert double action pocket army revolver with its birds-head grip. Antonio took the shotgun yet held it with disdain.

Mateo wanted to pretend to be the judge but Park insisted he must go, regardless of the risk. 'I must be a witness to this. It is my duty.'

'Very well,' Mateo conceded. 'Then, you shall be accompanied.' He turned to his wife. 'Josefa, would you take the risk?'

She smiled. 'I don't think it will be a big risk. I cannot see them killing a circuit judge.'

'They've already killed my pa,' Emmett reminded her.

'The boy has a point,' argued Judge Park. 'I'll be all right, I'm sure. There's no need for you to come with me, ma'am.'

Josefa shook her head. 'No, Mateo is correct. I'll be more useful in the town.' She slipped behind their wagon and changed into her skirt and blouse. When she stepped out, she said, 'I'll be travelling with you, Judge, but we won't know each other; just strangers on the stage. All right?'

Appraising her appreciatively, he nodded. 'Of course.'

On the roof of the coach, Ramón apologized and niftily opened the judge's trunk.

'My Lord, how'd you do that?' Judge Park fished in his vest pocket, pulled out the keys.

'It's what I do.' Ramón removed clothing and books and passed them down to Juan and Arcadia, who put them in the Mendoza wagon. 'I'm sorry for the inconvenience, sir, but I need sufficient room for my body.'

Gene and Emmett stared in admiration as Ramón folded

himself inside the trunk, closed the lid and clicked it shut. The boys were then hidden in the boot of the coach. Antonio bundled his two rifles in a blanket, hefted them up to the driver's box and shoved the roll out of sight. For now, the stage driver and shotgun would travel in the Mendoza wagon.

Chad, the guard at the bordello, detailed off a man to watch the salon while he, Trampas and three off-duty men forced themselves on the girls. Reluctantly the girls took them upstairs. That left two, Daisy and April, Madame Larkin mused. She looked at their new guard, a thin man of perhaps eighteen summers. 'What's your name, son?'

'Marvin, ma'am.'

'Well, Marvin,' she said, pointing to Daisy and April, 'don't you fancy the delights of one of my beauties?' She arched an eyebrow, jiggled her chest and swayed her hips.

Quick on the uptake, both Daisy and April looked coyly at Marvin.

He shook his head. 'No, thanks . . . I'm not really that way inclined.'

Great, Helen mused, just our luck!

The hostage townswomen made disapproving sounds in their corner and averted their eyes, while Matt the telegrapher smirked, his cheeks quite flushed.

Marvin cleared his throat. 'I'm sorry we're inconveniencing you and your business, ma'am.'

'That's all right, son. You've gotta do what your boss says, I guess.'

'Well, I must say, it is far from all right!' snapped one of the women hostages.

'Now, Thelma,' said a companion, 'Miss Larkin's just trying to be civilized.'

'I don't know how you can defend that woman!'

Madame Larkin smiled. 'I make a darned fine cup of java. Do you all want one?'

'Yeah,' Marvin said, 'I'd appreciate it, ma'am.'

'Please,' said Matt and then the four women nodded.

Daisy stood up. 'I'll make it.'

Madame Larkin held up her hand. 'No, dear, you relax while you can.' God knows what's in store for you later, she thought but didn't voice. 'I won't be a minute.'

In the kitchen, she wondered if she should dig out the shotgun hidden under her bed. No, not yet. There were more subtle ways to deal with these men. She rooted in the cupboards and, behind the molasses and tobacco, she found the tin of sleeping draught. She had enough to send an army to sleep if she so desired. The concoction came in handy when a few clients felt inclined to be difficult or even violent with one of the girls. A generous nightcap of whiskey with a little addition usually did the trick. It left an almighty hangover so they never suspected they'd been drugged. For a fleeting moment she considered administering it to those four sanctimonious townswomen.

Marvin seemed like a nice boy. But if she could drug him, maybe Daisy and April could get away. The rest of his pals probably couldn't count anyway and wouldn't miss the girls when they came down.

José was very tense as they hadn't anticipated that they'd get an escort to the livery, inside of which sat the man called Tully. Now, with Antonio beside him again riding shotgun, José followed Tully's directions and drove the stagecoach to Dent's livery at the far end of the street. He noticed the church on his right as he pulled up outside the shut doors of the livery. He leaned over the side, called, 'Tully, nobody's here. Will you open up?'

'Yeah, sure.' Tully stepped down and swung wide the big doors.

José drove the coach inside, enveloped by welcome shade and relatively cool air, and halted. 'I'll be glad to get me some shut-eye!' he said, elbowing Antonio in the ribs.

'Yeah, me too!' Antonio agreed and climbed down.

'Let's get the horses seen to first.'

'Aye,' said Antonio, 'if we can keep our eyes open!' Don't overdo it, my friend, José thought.

'While you do that, I'll go out and have a smoke,' Tully said. He swung one door shut, left the other open and lit his quirly as he went.

Quickly, Antonio lifted the flap of the boot and let out Gene and Emmett. 'Hide in the stalls for now,' he whispered, directing them.

No sooner did the boys get out of sight than Tully returned. 'Do you want a hand with the horses?'

'The sooner we do that, the sooner we can get that shut-eye,' said Antonio.

José laughed.

'What's so funny?' Antonio said.

José winked. 'You and your over-acting.'

Standing next to them, Tully gaped. 'Acting, what's—?'

José swung a roundhouse at Tully's nose.

Tully jerked backwards but he didn't fall. He staggered, wiped a hand on his bleeding nose and blinked, looking confused.

José dived at Tully and they both sprawled in the straw, very close to where Emmett and Gene hid, trading blows with their fists. Antonio leaped on the pair and rammed a cloth in Tully's mouth. He struggled, as if suffocating, but his nose was clear. Tully jerked and suddenly went into a spasm, then shuddered and was still.

'You were supposed to knock him out!' Antonio grated. 'Now look at him!'

José knelt by Tully and shook his head. 'I broke his nose – he couldn't breathe with your gag in his mouth.'

Antonio shrugged. 'It was an accident.'

Then the pair of them dragged Tully's body to a stall at the far end of the livery, out of sight.

Hardly affected by their exertion, they brushed off straw from their borrowed clothes.

Antonio shrugged. 'I had hoped you would knock him out. I had to use the gag, he was about to shout.'

'Don't dwell on it,' José said. 'I'm sure he wouldn't have worried if it had been the other way around.'

Antonio nodded. 'I would have hit him, but I have to think of my hands. They are needed.'

'You're probably right.' José rubbed his knuckles. 'A shame, he was a helpful man.'

'At least that's one less to worry about – one in return for the poor sheriff.'

'True.' José turned and whispered to the boys, 'It's safe to come out now.'

They emerged from their hiding place, straw sticking out of collars, cuffs and pockets.

'Did you see what happened?' Antonio asked them.

'Yes, sir. It wasn't your fault,' said Emmett. 'That was some punch, Mr Mendoza; if he hadn't been so big, you'd have floored him.'

'Thank you. Yes, it was, wasn't it?'

'What do we do now?' Gene asked.

'You both stay here and wait for your friends tonight,' said Antonio.

Gene eyed the stall, Tully's last resting place.

'It cannot be helped,' Antonio said. 'You must stay here and keep safe. Meanwhile, I'll get my weapons of choice ready.' He climbed up to the driver's box and hefted his blanket bundle.

'Hold it right there!'

José swung round. The back door of the livery had been opened without a sound and a man stood on the threshold, a shotgun levelled on them all.

'Don't try for your gun, mister!' snarled the man, 'or I'll blast you to hell!' He stepped forward a couple of paces and a light beam shone on his weather-beaten features and grey-blue eyes. 'Now, who in tarnation are you? You sure ain't the regular coach crew!'

'Mr Dent!' Emmett exclaimed.

'Emmett?' Dent opened his snaggle-toothed mouth in surprise.

Emmett ran forward, quite recklessly, thought José. Then the boy stopped in front of the man with the shotgun and said, 'I've brought these people to help us!'

'Is that so? All two of them, eh?' He lowered the shotgun and chuckled. 'You fellows must be real crack shots if you reckon you can take back our town.'

'I'm a sharpshooter, Mr Dent,' said Antonio from the top of the coach, 'but even I would find it difficult to outshoot so many desperados.'

'How have you got a shotgun, sir?' José asked. 'Emmett tells us all the guns were confiscated.'

'The boy's telling the truth.' Dent clasped a hand on Emmett's shoulder. 'I hid my trusty greener in the straw when I saw what was happening. I let them take my Navy Colt to keep them happy.'

'Mr Dent owns the livery,' Emmett explained. 'His wife runs the eatery.'

Later, while José got a little sleep and Antonio set up his

weapons in the loft, Dent let in Alice, Maura and Eric. Then Dent left the children to it and went out the back, on lookout. The children sat on straw in a stall adjacent to Tully's and sat open-mouthed as Gene and Emmett related their adventure.

Urging the others to silence, Emmett reached into his shirt and pulled out a six-gun.

'Where'd you get that?' Gene whispered.

Emmett thumbed at the next stall. 'The man named Tully dropped it in the fight. Maybe it fell out of his holster. Anyway, it slid under the straw and I found it – and kept it.'

'It's dangerous,' Alice said.

'You're too young to have a gun,' berated Maura.

Emmett shrugged. 'Finders keepers, I reckon.'

Maura shook her head. 'I say you should give it to the circus men – or Mr Dent.'

'No, he's right,' Alice said. 'Finders is keepers.' She eyed him seriously. 'But be careful, Emmett. I've heard of kids shooting themselves or their brothers or sisters by accident.'

'Yeah, I'll be careful.' He slid the heavy gun under his shirt.

Juan halted the wagon at the foot of the mountain, to the west of town. 'We'll not be gone long,' he told the stage driver and shotgun.

'No problem, mister,' said the driver. 'We can use the rest.'

Slowly, Juan climbed up with Arcadia by his side.

At the top, they lowered themselves to the ground and crawled along, and carefully edged forward until they reached the lip of the overhang. They looked down on the mine and Conejos Blancos.

Miners moved about the compound, pushing carts, hefting buckets of dark-coloured ore. Directly below them, some twenty-five feet, there was the gaping cave entrance and on the broad lip stood the winch gear, which was fully rigged and working. Accompanied by a creaking noise, a bucket of pure silver ore trundled jerkily down the cable to the base collection point, where it was emptied and stacked, ready for the smelter. Three wagons idled nearby.

Juan peered to the left, concealed behind an outcrop of rock. 'I see four miners in the cave.'

'And the guards for the mine,' Arcadia pointed out. 'One in each watchtower.'

'Two. Yes. The information the boys gave us seems accurate.'

He studied the town. Everything looked quite normal – until he studied the people in more detail. Yes, there on the street corner by the bank was a sentry with a shotgun. And the guard by the jail. He glimpsed the guards outside the town hall, those by the bridge, at the mine compound gate, but that was all. It was an incomplete picture but it tallied with what Emmett and Gene had divulged.

He eased away from the rim and signed for Arcadia to follow him back down.

When they reached the wagon, they found the two stage men fast asleep. Soundlessly, they removed what they needed, filled two bags and strapped them to their backs. Juan also looped a length of rope over his shoulder and carried two lengths of wood.

Time to climb the mountainside.

Once at the top, they lowered everything to the ground and sat quite still.

'This is the hard part,' Juan said. 'We must all wait until night falls.'

CHAPTER 7

TIGHTROPE

Mid-afternoon seemed a good time for the coach to leave town, José reckoned, the crew having supposedly enjoyed a few hours of rest. He climbed up the ladder to the loft and said, 'We'll go now, *amigo*. See you when all hell breaks loose, eh?'

Antonio, comfortably ensconced in the livery loft, with his Sharps Borchardt 1878 rifle and a Winchester by his side, turned and smiled. He commanded an excellent view down Main Street and over the rooftops, with a direct line of sight to the town hall steps. From here, too, he could cover the entrance to the bordello on the right and in fact the length of Hallahan Road. '*Sí, amigo*. Go with God.'

José nodded, crossed himself then climbed down and mounted the stagecoach. Alongside him sat Gene, wearing the shirt, vest and hat Antonio had arrived in. A minor detail, José mused, but perhaps one of the desperados would notice a change in attire. Antonio wore Tully's shirt, since he had no call for it.

Dent opened the doors and José urged the team forward, out into Hallahan Road. He glanced to the right, noting the sentry to the bordello, then urged the horses forward and round the corner, heading for the southern end of town, past the church and smithy on his right and the tannery to the left. Ahead, the town limits, identified by a population notice – and the cholera warning sign.

He reckoned he'd keep on going until the coach was out of sight about a mile away, behind a large boulder – not far from the gorge. Plenty of time.

Blake's first stop was the Tanglefoot Saloon, where he ordered a bottle of bourbon to celebrate his freedom.

The bartender was about to ask for payment then, seeing that Blake was armed, closed his mouth. 'It's on the house, sir.'

'Smart decision,' Blake said with a sneer. 'There's no law in this town to protect you now.' He downed the drink and let out a sigh then a belch. 'That barely touched the sides, but it sure hit home!'

He topped up the glass and turned, leaning his back against the counter, while he studied the room.

The piano player was idle, dozing in a corner. Two tables – four men at each – indulged in poker; the pots at the centre were small, penny ante stuff, not worth his time. A young cowpoke stood at the far end of the bar, staring into his beer.

'Hey, cowboy, come over, share a drink with me!' he called, his voice booming. Despite the loudness, nobody at the tables seemed to notice.

The cowboy glanced up, glancing around. 'You talking to me?'

'Yes, you. Now, come here. I don't like drinking alone.'

'Sure, sir.' The cowboy walked up to Blake, carrying his half-empty beer glass.

'Finish that off and have some real booze, son.'

'Don't mind if I do.' He downed the rest of his beer and slid the glass to the barman; it was replaced with a shot glass. 'Name's Chip, sir.'

'Monty,' said Blake as he poured. Then he handed it over and refilled his own. He lifted his glass. 'A toast, Chip – to freedom!'

'Yeah, I'll drink to that.'

'You don't sound too pleased. What's eating you?'

'Well, I promised my girl Lizzie I wouldn't join Grant's gang again – now look, here I am.'

Blake chuckled. 'Your girl shouldn't rule your life, son. You've only got the one life, so you live it – don't let someone else make you live it like they want. You live it like you want!'

Chip downed the bourbon and smiled. 'Say, that sounds like pretty good advice, Monty.'

'Yeah, it does, don't it?' He was surprised at himself. 'Here, have another drink.'

'Too much booze?' Hotelier Darnell Grady wondered, massaging his chest as he stood behind the reception counter. From here, he could see into the bar lounge where Hart's men made free with the spirits. They were drinking all the profits and he didn't expect any payment would be forthcoming. Maybe that's what caused the stabbing pain in his chest? It couldn't be anything serious, he reckoned; for God's sake, he was only fifty-five! Yet he recalled examining his blood-shot eyes in the mirror this morning and he wondered where his double chin had suddenly come from, too.

One of the desperados sashayed up to him. 'Hey, we're running short on beer. You got any down your cellar?'

Grady bit his lip. Instead of telling the uncouth man to go to hell, he nodded. 'Surely, sir,' his voice quite squeaky. 'But I'd appreciate it if you would carry the barrel up the stairs for me.'

'Hell, no problem – we're drinking it, ain't we?'

'Yes, you certainly are.' Grady stepped out from the counter and led the way down a corridor and turned left into a poorly lit alcove. He pointed to a door set in the wall. 'The cellar's through here.' He withdrew a key, unlocked the door and pulled it back. He picked up a lantern off a hook on the wall and lit it, then shone its light through the doorway. Stairs led downwards.

He handed the man the lantern. 'You go first.'

The man took the light, swayed a little, then stepped over the threshold.

Grady hastily checked left and right then kicked with all his might, which was considerable, considering the extra weight he carried. The flat of his foot hit the man squarely on the seat of his pants and before he could utter a sound he was tumbled head-over-heels down the stairs. 'Oh, dear me!' Grady exclaimed and hastened down.

The man's neck was broken.

He hurried upstairs and rushed into the bar area and grabbed the first man he came to, explained there'd been an accident.

This man shrugged. 'He should've stuck to spirits. Beer ain't good for you.' Then he turned back to his glass of brandy.

'Oh, right,' said Grady. 'Well, I'd better get the undertaker.'

'Yeah, you do that.' The man hiccupped. 'Seems like my share of the silver just increased.'

Two more of Hart's men met unfortunate accidents. One fell down a wishing well near the church – some said their wish had been granted – and another was crushed under falling timber as he passed a half-completed dwelling. Still, the attrition rate wasn't high enough to cause the desperados any concern.

'You've no need to worry, Mrs Rosco,' Alice said. 'Emmett and Gene are all right. They're back in town but they can't come home just yet.'

Resting a concerned hand on Hayley's shoulder, Alden said, 'Why can't they come home?' His tone was stern; a fiery temper was being stoked not far from the surface.

Alice shrugged. 'It's a secret. I swore not to say. But I wanted to tell you not to worry.' She stood up, moved away from the sofa. 'Now I've told you, I'd better be going.'

Alden was tempted to grab Alice's arm and shake the truth out of her. But Hayley's hand on his tempered him. Stress, he supposed. It was getting to all of us.

As Alice let herself out, he turned to Hayley. 'It's all very well her telling us not to worry, but since . . . well, I'm . . . Gene's all I've got.'

Hayley patted his hand. 'They're sensible boys, Alden. I'm sure they know what they're doing.' She smiled up at him. 'You'll see, it will be all right.' Tears glinted in her eyes.

Ramón finally received a response from the fort. A troop of cavalry was already out on patrol. They were not due to report in by telegraph until tomorrow at noon. Once they did so, they would be redirected to Conejos Blancos. It was estimated that the cavalry wouldn't arrive for at least two days, however.

He sighed. This changed everything. Should they pull back and wait? They had no evidence of any more deaths. Why put the entire Mendoza troupe at risk? It was the cavalry's job, after all. Doubts pestered him. If only he could talk to Mateo!

He glanced over at Theo, who lay tethered and gagged among the luggage, the curtain drawn back so he stayed visible. He didn't think any of Hart's men would come here. Though they might miss Theo. Unless . . . was he due for relief at any time?

Ramón stood and crossed the room, the bolas dangling at his hip, and removed Theo's gag. 'Tell me, are you expecting anyone to relieve you here?'

Theo licked his lips, swallowed. 'No. I'm the only one trained to use the telegraph.'

'Good.' Ramón moved to pull the gag into place again.

Theo pulled his head back, shied away. 'Wait, what about grub? I'm starving!'

'A fair point. My stomach rumbles also. What are the feeding arrangements?'

'The restaurant owner drops off food for me on her way to the town hall.'

'When?'

'Midday, and again at about six.'

'Then you must wait until midday, I think.' He shoved the gag on.

There was a slight risk. What was the restaurant owner's name? The boy mentioned her. Ah, yes, Mrs Dent. She might not be able to keep it secret that Theo was a captive.

It was going to be a long day.

Once the business concerning the day's food was out of the way, he must wait through the night until it was dawn and then he would join Mateo, as planned. He peered out the window – not far to run to the town hall. But it seemed a great distance in the daylight. Dawn seemed a long way off.

Once he'd driven the stage out of town, José drew the team to a halt behind a large boulder, not far from the narrow Parnham Gorge.

In readiness, he uncoupled the horses from the central tongue and ground hobbled them.

Then they sat inside the coach and waited.

'What are we waiting for, Mr Mendoza?' Gene asked.

'Dawn.'

'And then what?'

'The Magnificent Mendozas begin what might be their final act. . . .'

In the bordello, Madame Larkin got Daisy and April to go upstairs with trays carrying five cups of steaming coffee. 'Make sure they drink it.' She turned, smiling all innocence at Marvin, 'And I'll prepare some food, as well.'

'Mighty decent of you, ma'am,' said Marvin, taking a cup. Then he put it down on a sideboard and paced the room, occasionally glancing at the stairs.

Madame Larkin wondered if he was tempted after all. Maybe she'd try again, when Daisy and April returned. She went into the kitchen.

A few minutes later, she was joined by Daisy and April. 'Two of them wouldn't take the coffee,' April said. 'All they want is whiskey and sex!'

Madame Larkin cursed under her breath. She should've laced the whiskey; she'd done that before. Wasn't thinking straight. Then she sighed, handed the plates of beef sandwiches to Daisy. 'See if young Marvin wants a bite to eat – before he nods off.' As an aside, she added, 'Well, we've probably only got two left to deal with. . . .'

Food issued by Mrs Dent was more substantial than sandwiches, and consisted of stewed steak, potatoes, beans and cabbage. As she delivered it using Lily's buckboard, she trembled any time she went near one of Hart's men. Most of them treated her civilly enough, but she couldn't get out of her head that they'd killed Tad Rosco and Mr Watzman.

It was a long day not only for her, but for many. Four off-duty sentries slept in the rooms above the Tanglefoot Saloon, another two slept in the Talbot Hotel, while the majority of the remainder preferred to play cards, drink or just relax in the

Rabbit's Hole Saloon.

Lily McKenzie was kept busy in the general store, though she didn't see any profits coming through the door. Her regular customers seemed shy to enter, perhaps because there was usually one or two of Hart's men skulking there.

'I'll take a packet of Bull Durham, ma'am,' Kendall said.

Tight-lipped, Lily took it from the shelf and handed it across the counter.

'How much, ma'am?'

Her dove grey eyes stared at him, as if he'd sprouted horns or maybe angels' wings. She brushed stray auburn hair from her creased brow. 'You want to pay?'

'Sure. This is a general store, after all.'

'But none of your men pay – they just take.'

Colour rose into his weathered cheeks. 'They what?'

'They got me to start a tab, but I heard from more than one of them that they'll never settle up.'

Behind Kendall, a young man was busy sweeping the floorboards, his broom creating little swirls of dust. He leaned in towards Kendall. 'Miss Lily's really worried, mister, about making ends meet. I can tell. She's lost all her colour.' He pointed directly at her face. Her normally wan complexion was now even pastier; perhaps it was mainly with worry.

'Johnny, that's nonsense!' Lily exclaimed, her cheeks reddening.

Johnny grinned widely, rolled his eyes and scooted out the front door, trailing his broom with him while humming a ditty.

Kendall grinned, unfolded a couple of bills from his vest pocket and dropped them on the counter. 'That should cover the tobacco, ma'am. I'll have words with Hart.'

'That's real fine of you. Thank you, Mr. . . ?'

'Kendall, ma'am. I don't hold with robbing honest working folk. And I can't see Mr Hart condoning it, either.'

'But the mine's this town's lifeblood.' She looked flustered, wringing her hands together, wiping them on her apron. 'I don't mean to rile you, Mr . . . Mr Kendall, but we rely on the miners, the businesses affected by the mine, and—'

Kendall held up a hand to still her tirade and shrugged. 'I can't help that, ma'am. But I sure as hell – sorry, ma'am – I sure won't stand for robbing storekeepers like your good self.' He tipped a finger at the brim of his hat. 'See you around, ma'am.'

He stepped out and embarked on making a quirly, then he turned right, intent on slaking his thirst at the Tanglefoot Saloon.

A few paces further down, Bernie Trevone, one of Kendall's men, bumped into young Johnny as he swept the boardwalk at the front of the store. 'Get the hell outta my way!' Bernie snarled.

'I was just, just . . .' Johnny mumbled.

'Just show respect to your betters!' Bernie clenched his fists. 'You look a bit simple, kid – maybe I'd be doing you a favour, putting you down like a rabid dog!'

Abruptly, he punched Johnny in the face.

The lad stumbled backwards, a hand to his bloody nose.

'Hey, that's no way to treat Johnny!' exclaimed Lily, rushing out. 'He's just a little slow, is all.'

'Slow, is he? Well, he needs to learn quick to keep outta people's way!' Bernie reached for his gun. 'I'll make the simpleton dance to my tune!'

The hammer of a revolver clicked next to Bernie's ear. 'I wouldn't do anything foolish, now, Bernie,' said Kendall, levelling his Colt Peacemaker.

Bernie moved his hand from his gun butt and slowly turned to face Kendall. 'What's it to you?' He sneered at Johnny. 'He's a worthless piece of—'

Suddenly, Kendall swiped his gun barrel across Bernie's

face, breaking skin. 'Get the hell away from here before I really lose my temper!'

Bernie fidgeted, his hand hovering over his gun butt. Then he wiped his bloody cheek and scowled. 'I'll remember this, Kendall.'

'Be sure you do. Remembering a little humanity wouldn't go amiss, either.'

Bernie sloped off, crossing the street, making a beeline for the Rabbit's Hole.

Kendall helped Johnny to his feet. 'Sorry about that, son.' He fished in his jeans pocket, gave the boy a handful of nickels. 'Maybe you can buy something in the store with that to make amends, huh?'

'Yes, mister, I can do that,' Johnny said.

Without another word, Kendall pivoted on his heel and walked along the boardwalk and entered the Tanglefoot Saloon, where he stayed for the rest of the day, nursing a single beer.

Mrs Dent was returning to her restaurant when the miners finished work. Normally, they would walk down to the town's saloons and have a few drinks before wending their way home or back to their quarters. But today, they seemed weary and in no mood to rub shoulders with their captors. With the shirts on their backs drenched in sweat, discoloured with dust, their grimy faces downcast and sullen, she reflected that they were reminiscent of paintings of the damned emerging from purgatory.

She couldn't blame them – they were working in dangerous conditions for the men who would rob them.

Night fell and both Juan and Arcadia changed into black leotards; they'd had to rub soil on the bright rhinestones that patterned them. Juan's Navy Colt was also smothered in dirt in case the gun metal glinted.

Juan's fob watch showed 3 a.m. He looped the rope around a boulder and used it to lower Arcadia to the cave entrance. Slung over her back was her bow and, tucked in the large quiver, arrows.

As she descended hand over hand, her mouth felt dry.

The sentries in both watchtowers seemed to be looking down at the miners' quarters, not here.

When Arcadia's feet touched the solid ground of the cave lip, she breathed easier.

She strung the bow and nocked a special arrow.

The distance wasn't too great. And she wasn't aiming at a little tinkling bell now.

She let loose and before the first arrow hit its target she was ready with the second.

The sentries in the watchtowers toppled over backwards as the lead arrow tips bludgeoned the temple of each man. She checked the sentry at the gate to the mine entrance. He paced in a slovenly fashion, and certainly wasn't alert. She'd heard the watchtower sentries tumble to the floor, but clearly the man at the gate hadn't. The shadows didn't give her a good shot, but she must attempt it.

Her third arrow found its mark and the gate sentry crumpled to the ground.

'Good work,' Juan whispered and passed down a length of wood with a wedge affixed two-thirds of the way up: one half of a pair of stilts.

She acknowledged him and then, with the aid of the stilt, climbed up on to the winch mechanism. There was a little grease, but not much; most of it was clogged with dust. That was why the movement of the bucket had been jerky earlier today, she reckoned. Still, the cable was taut as it dropped at an angle towards the unloading section. Hauling up the stilt, she placed her left foot forward at a slight angle, her big toe feeling the thickness of the cable. She was surprised; unlike a tightrope, the braided steel cable was about five inches wide and almost an inch thick – in fact, harder to walk on.

Balance. Steady. Not as much give as a tightrope, either.

She used the stilt as a balancing pole and, slowly, carefully, she walked down the cable, concentrating ahead, not looking down, inching forward one step at a time.

Finally, she reached the bottom of the winch and used the stilt to help her to the ground. Her landing was almost soundless.

Here, at the base, was the steam engine that worked the winch, and a wagonload of silver, virtually ready for transporting.

While Arcadia nocked an arrow and kept lookout, Juan walked down the cable using the second stilt for balance.

When he reached her side, they moved towards the miners' quarters. There was only a single door, so she guessed the sleeping arrangements were in dormitories, perhaps, running the length of the building. A variety of snores came from several open windows that glowed with a buttery light. 'You'd better do the talking,' Arcadia whispered. 'They will not listen to a woman – and a Mexican at that.'

Juan chuckled, because she usually called the shots and coordinated their act. He was happy to let her take the lead. And she enjoyed it. 'I'll try, my dear.'

He opened the door.

The room was lined with ten bunks, all occupied. A single lantern hung from the ceiling, bathing the place in its weak yellow glow.

Two men sat at a square table under the light, playing cards; Juan groaned inwardly as he recognized one of them: Shanley

Donnelly, the Mexican-hater who'd fought Ignacio, was unmistakable with his skin like the sole of an old boot, and his misshapen nose like an Idaho potato. They both stopped playing and looked up at Juan and Arcadia.

'*Buenas tardes,*' Juan said, bowing slightly.

'Hey, it's one of those Mexes from the circus!' the other card player exclaimed.

In ones and twos, the sleeping miners woke, raised themselves from their bunks, some complaining about the time.

Juan put a finger to his mouth. 'Not so loud, *señor*. We don't want the very bad gringos in the office to hear.'

Donnelly threw down his cards, stood up, scraped back his chair and stepped forward. 'What are you doing here?' His lips held a sneer and his sandy-coloured eyes glared.

'We've come to rescue you – and the townspeople.'

Donnelly rested his fists on his hips and laughed. 'You and whose army?'

'There are others – from the circus,' Arcadia said.

Only wearing his underwear, Sheldon McTavish pushed in front of Donnelly, his soot-coloured eyes wide, showing worry. 'But the – the hostages . . . my wife's one of them!' His rasping voice rose, his soup-strainer moustache wafting as he spoke. 'I don't think it's a good idea to antagonize Hart and his men.'

'It's too late for that,' Juan said. 'We need your help.' He thumbed at Arcadia. 'My wife has knocked out the sentries in the watchtowers and at the gate.'

Someone whistled and was hastily silenced.

Another whispered, 'That's some woman!'

A few concurred, eyeing Arcadia's body-clinging leotard.

'What do you want us to do?' Donnelly asked; a tone of respect in his voice now.

'Find something to tie up the sentries. And gag them. We don't want them to raise the alarm.'

'Thank God for that,' murmured McTavish.

Donnelly gave him a hard stare and turned back to Juan. 'Then what?'

'We'll break into the mining office and free the hostages in there.'

'The stairs to the office creak – they'll hear you coming,' Donnelly said.

'We're prepared for that.' Juan winked at Arcadia.

'Just – just the two of you?' McTavish's voice quavered.

'Mr Donnelly and one other can assist,' Juan said, adding with a shrug, 'if you wish.'

'You're on, pal.' Donnelly swivelled round, studying the men.

'I'll go,' McTavish said.

'Sorry.' Donnelly shook his head. 'I reckon you're a tad too old.'

'I'm only fifty-two.'

'And I'm over ten years younger than you, Sheldon.' Donnelly pointed at a young man with ginger hair. 'Jamie, you're with me. OK, lads, let's get ready for some action!'

'But do it quietly,' Arcadia said urgently. 'We still have the town to consider.'

'Yes, she's right,' McTavish added grumpily.

The men quickly dressed. When Donnelly had organized men to obtain rope and material to tie and gag the sentries, he retrieved the rifle from the unconscious man at the gate. Then with Jamie, the red-headed miner, he joined Juan beneath the balcony of the mine-owner's office.

With Juan's aid, Arcadia mounted the pair of stilts, teetered for a few seconds and then walked towards the balcony.

The rail was about a foot higher than her head, but she could just about reach up and grab one of the posts. When she was sure it would take her weight, she kicked away the stilts and

Juan caught them, lowered them quietly to the ground. She eased herself up the balcony and silently slid over the rail. She peered down. Donnelly and Jamie watched.

Juan threw her the rope and she tied it to the balcony rail. He hauled himself up, followed quickly by the two miners.

Arcadia heard voices, but it was impossible to determine how many people were inside. And the boy hadn't known, since he wasn't given access to the mine compound. She beckoned to Donnelly.

Carrying the rifle, he crossed the wooden boards and leaned close to her and she got a waft of his body odour.

'Do you know how many of Hart's men are inside?' she whispered.

'Don't know for sure. I saw two, and Hart and his girlfriend – a nasty piece with a gun.'

She eyed Juan. 'Eight hostages – and four gunmen.'

Juan shrugged. 'We must do this, *chica*.'

CHAPTER 8

'POOR INNOCENT RICH GIRL'

Pat woke in the sheriff's chair with a stiff neck. He glanced at the wall clock and swore: twenty after three, goddamn it! He eased off the chair and lit another oil lamp, then carried it across the room and glanced through the open door into the jail area. He was surprised to see that none of his prisoners were sleeping. The woman and the judge sat on opposite bunks in one cell. Deputy Sheriff Leavy and two other towns-men sat in the other.

He liked the look of the filly, but could bide his time.

His stomach rumbled. He wondered if that woman's grub had been tampered with, maybe even poisoned. Nah, she wouldn't have the guts. He belched, and his insides churned. He needed to go to the outhouse, pronto.

He put the lantern on the desk, strode hurriedly to the door, opened it and stepped out on to the porch.

The privy was round the back. On his way, he pulled out the makings and lit a quirly.

*

In her cell, Josefa turned to Judge Park and signed for him to keep silent as she fiddled with her hair and withdrew a small sliver of metal. 'A lock-pick,' she whispered, 'courtesy of Ramón before we boarded the stage.'

He smiled wryly and nodded. Then his eyes shone as she stood and placed a foot on her bunk; her skirt fell away from her leg and she removed a throwing knife from her boot.

She hefted it, and it seemed that its handle was quite weighty.

By now, the others had noticed and she put a finger to her lips. Deputy Leavy had a better view through the open doorway into the office area. She pointed to her eye, signed for him to keep a lookout. He nodded.

Sliding the knife into the waistband at her back, she leaned through the bars and applied the pick to the lock. Sweat beaded her forehead as she manipulated the sliver of metal. Ramón had instructed her a few times; it always looked easy when he attempted it. Her wet fingers slipped, but she retained her grip. Damned awkward cuss, she fumed.

Emily Chase yawned and said, 'Light another blasted lamp, Jesse.' She gestured at the mine owner, Simeon Gray, his daughter, Janet McTavish, the wife of the shoe-smith and four townsmen, all clustered in the corner at the other side of Gray's desk. 'I don't want our hostages slinking off into the shadows!'

'Why me, Emmy?' said one of two guards who accompanied her. He was swarthy, and had a squint.

'Don't get familiar with me. It's Miss Chase to you.'

Jesse leaned against the wall and folded his arms. 'You do it, Coburn, I'm not keen on taking orders from no woman – a mere girl, at that!'

'Awright, keep your hair on,' snapped Coburn. He removed his cigarette, blew on its tip till it was bright red and then used it to light the wick of the nearest oil lamp on the desk, next to a bucket of drinking water and a tin mug. He then went to the door and turned up the lantern hanging there.

Emily glared at Jesse. 'You wait, I'll tell the boss and he'll cut you down to size!'

Jesse swore colourfully at her.

Simeon Gray stepped forward, barked, 'Please, let's calm down. There's no cause for all this unpleasantness. Our situation is bad enough as it is!'

Emily swung round on him and then scowled at Naomi, who clung to her father's arm. 'Poor innocent rich girl! I hear you fancied that circus sharpshooter – they say he's quite the ladies' man!' She laughed coarsely.

Simeon turned to study Naomi. 'Is this right? Have you been seeing that circus man, even though I forbade it?'

'Antonio,' she said, blushing. 'He has a name, Father.'

Emily's cackling laughter froze in her throat as the door was kicked in by Jamie.

Arcadia hastily took in the scene and let fly an arrow at one guard, Coburn, the lead arrowhead hitting him in the temple, knocking him unconscious.

In the same instant, Naomi let go of her father and jumped at Emily and they tumbled to the floor, wrestling and scratching, pulling at each other's hair and clothes. A sleeve of Naomi's blouse was torn off at the seams.

Emily attempted to withdraw her six-gun but Naomi brutally restrained her.

'Don't think about making a move,' Donnelly said as he jacked a bullet in his raised rifle. 'Lower your gun-belt.' He eyed Jesse and cast an amused glance at the wrestling females.

Jesse nervously obeyed.

'I hate to break up such an intimate get-together,' Jamie said, leaning down. With an effort, he separated the two fighting women.

The front of Emily's shirt had been ripped. Taking his eyes off her, Jamie roughly pushed Emily to stand beside Jesse. 'Miss Naomi, are you OK?' he asked solicitously.

Brushing hair from her face, her lower lip trembling, Naomi nodded. Her father stepped forward and drew her to him, casting a burning glare at Emily.

Juan scanned the room and demanded, 'Where's Hart? Is there another room?'

Emily stared insolently at Naomi, her hand hovering over her holster.

Naomi boldly left her father's arms, stepped forward, slapped Emily and swiftly pulled Emily's six-gun. She backed off, cocking the weapon and aiming it.

Simeon moved alongside her and gently lowered the gun. 'Hart went to the town hall,' he said.

'OK,' Arcadia said. 'Tie them up.' Then she stepped out on to the balcony and lit the touch-paper of an attachment to an arrow. As it fizzed, sparkling, she shot it into the night sky.

The firework was silent as it spread its spray of silver and red stars – ephemeral, but it was the agreed signal.

Josefa had unlocked the cell door and tiptoed out, through the jailhouse door. If she could get the keys, it would be easier than trying to lock-pick the other cell.

At that moment, Pat reached the doorway, smoking, one of his suspenders still dangling at his hip. Abruptly, he straightened and looked skyward. 'What the hell?'

Josefa was halfway across the room when she saw it, too, the firework's cascading arc in the night sky.

Pat swung round, entered the office and started, surprised.

Josefa was about six feet away from him, approaching. She carried a knife. 'Hell!'

He grabbed for his gun and dived to one side.

She threw the knife, but miscalculated, due to his sudden movement. Instead of the heavy knife butt slamming into his forehead, the blade sank into his right arm. He shrieked out loud, dropped the six-gun and tumbled to the floorboards.

Swiftly, she ran over and kicked the gun away, knelt beside him, withdrew the blade and slammed the knife butt against his temple.

He stopped wailing.

'Damn,' she whispered, noticing she had his blood on her blouse.

She got to her feet, hurried to the doorway. Nobody seemed to have heard Pat's cries, thanks be to God.

Darkness smothered the town hall and the surrounding area that approached near the bridge, while cloud obscured the full moon.

Mateo slunk in from the north. Crouching as he moved, he paused as the firework signal lit the sky.

The mine was secure – well done, Arcadia, Juan!

The two sentries at the bridge entrance also noticed the pyrotechnic display. In that same instant, while they were distracted, Mateo used the heavy handle of his knife to knock out the nearest sentry, and then threw a second knife the length of the bridge to incapacitate the other, who crumpled to the ground. He dragged the first unconscious man across the rough boards of the bridge then tied up both of them with strips of leather he'd brought especially. Their bandannas served as gags.

Leaving his captives in a bunch of reeds by the edge of the bridge entrance, Mateo stepped out on to Mine Street.

He breathed easier when he noticed Ramón emerging from the telegraph office. He'd seen the signal too. The plan was working, so far.

Ramón stepped down from the boardwalk and, his bolas dangling at his hip, crossed the junction, heading towards the town hall steps at the top of which stood a solitary sentry whose name, according to the two boys, was Bret.

Bret noticed Ramón's approach and scuffled down a few steps. 'Hey,' he shouted, 'who the hell are you?'

This stopped Ramón in his tracks. Wisely, he didn't make any threatening gestures. 'I'm lost, *señor*!' he called, raising his hands in the air.

'Lost? Hey, you're a Mex—'

Mateo had his chance and used his knife again, aiming the butt at Bret's forehead. But it didn't quite work this time and it only thudded into his cheek.

Bret stumbled on the bottom step, drew his gun, and shot at Ramón.

Ramón sank to one knee, a hand grasping his wounded left arm.

Before he could recover completely and let loose any more lead, Bret staggered back against the steps, suddenly shot in the leg and the right arm. Before Bret could shout out, Mateo quickly disarmed him, and then knocked him out with his own gun butt.

Mateo glanced up the dark street illuminated at intervals by lamps and glimpsed the livery loft at the far end. He grinned and waved to Antonio, even though he couldn't see him.

Damn. He rushed over to Ramón, helped him to stand. 'Can you still do it?' he asked.

'*Sí, sí.*' Ramón nodded and spoke through gritted teeth. 'I'll live – show me where the explosives are . . . and I'll defuse them.'

As Mateo led Ramón round the back of the town hall, he sighed. The element of surprise was lost at the sound of those shots. The chances of no killing were seriously reduced.

CHAPTER 9

THE KILLINGS BEGIN

Standing at the Tanglefoot bar, Monty Blake was still celebrating his freedom with a bottle of bourbon when the shooting began. He lowered his glass, straightened. 'What's going on?' he asked Chip, who was leaning next to him.

'I'll take a look.'

Chip went, peered over the batwings and turned, hollered, 'There's a sniper up in the livery – he's cut down Bret already!'

'I thought you had the town sewn up tight?'

'Well, obviously somebody didn't attend the sewing bee!'

'No need to get shirty, Chip.' Blake swallowed his drink, straightened his gun-belt. 'Let's nip out the back, see what we can do to even things up.'

'Yeah, OK.'

The pair hurried to the rear of the saloon.

Blake opened the door, glanced out. Nobody occupied North Street; it was too early for anyone to be about, let alone hear the shots. He pulled out his revolver. 'Come on, we've got a clear run to the end of the street.'

The two of them stepped down to the hardpan. There was no boardwalk on this side. Opposite was the fruit and vegetable shop, the carpenter and at the far corner the funeral parlour. There, at the crossroads, he reckoned they'd be most vulnerable. He'd worry about that when he got there.

The fire from the livery was continuous – not hasty, just persistent, as if the shooter was determined to keep the heads of Hart's men down. As Blake approached the shoe-smith on his right, the funeral parlour on his left, he stopped suddenly.

Chip bumped into him. 'What the. . . ?'

Blake saw the shape of a man emerging from the funeral home, saw the glint of metal, and fired.

The man crumpled to the boardwalk.

Pistol drawn and cocked, Chip ran over and knelt down. 'Shit, you've shot the undertaker!'

'He was carrying a gun!'

Chip held up a cane, its silver handle glinting in the light of the overhead street lamp.

In that instant, Chip jerked back against the wall of the funeral parlour, a dark stain spreading across his chest. 'Oh, shit . . . oh, Lizzie. . . .'

Blake rushed to the corner of the shoe-smith and swore. His element of surprise was lost. The shooter must have seen the glint of the cane and surmised the same, that it was a weapon, and fired. Hell, he was a good shot, to hit his mark in this poor light. It looked like Lizzie's beau had thrown in his chips.

He fired at the corner lamp; the glass shattered and the light flickered out. Hunkering down, he decided he'd wait till the opportunity was right before he'd make his move against the marksman.

In the bordello, Marvin was already on his feet, although a little unsteady, the instant he heard the shooting. He shook his head, feeling a mite groggy. The shots echoed so he couldn't tell where they came from – maybe the other end of town. He gaped at the sight of two men – Trampas and Chad – rushing down the staircase, half-dressed, suspenders dangling, over-shirts undone. Six-guns drawn, they used a girl each as shields and hurried through the foyer.

'What's going on, Marv?' Chad asked, limping as his foot wasn't settled properly in his right boot.

'All I know is I heard shots.' Marvin shrugged. He eyed the two girls. 'Leave them girls be, Chad!' He moved to block their progress.

'Shoot, you're a real pain!' Chad growled and raised his six-gun, shot Marvin.

Marvin tumbled backwards, upsetting his coffee cup. Pain stabbing his side, he sank to one knee.

Chad glared at Madame Larkin. 'Where are the others – Tom, Hal and Chris?' he demanded.

She shrugged. 'Sleeping it off with my girls, I shouldn't wonder. Seems the safest place to be right now, by the sound of it.'

Storming across the room, his six-gun raised, he pointed the barrel at her temple. 'Nowhere's safe if I'm around,' he grated.

Abruptly, he coughed, stared at her in surprise and stumbled sideways, the top half of his head blasted off. The sound of the six-gun seemed to linger.

Then the wailing of the four hostage townswomen started.

Her face and chest blood-splattered, Madame Larkin shouted, 'Shut the hell up!'

Abruptly, the women went silent, eyes wide in shock.

Madame Larkin stared at Marvin.

With one hand he grasped his wounded side, the other shook with the weight of his smoking pistol. He snarled, 'Get the hell out, Trampas – but don't take any girls!'

Thrusting the girls aside, Trampas raised his hands and sidled to the exit doors. 'I'm going, I'm going.' He winked at the blonde girl he'd brought down the stairs. 'Thanks, Charlene, you're a treasure!'

He opened the door.

Charlene stood, hands to her chest, her eyes tear-brimmed. She raised a hand, faintly waved.

Trampas rushed out, slammed the door.

Seconds later, Marvin tumbled sideways to the floor. Instantly, he was surrounded by sweet-smelling women, concerned about his wound.

'Where are. . . ?' he managed.

'Here, have some coffee. It'll help while we take care of your bloody side,' said Madame Larkin, producing a fresh cup.

'You sure I should drink. . . ?'

'It's superficial, son. You ain't gut-shot.'

He swallowed the brew. 'That's nice.'

'Good lad. Your other three pals are drugged and well out of it.'

'But. . . ?' He slumped, unconscious.

'Come on, girls, let's get him to my room.' As Madame Larkin slept on the ground floor, there were no stairs to negotiate. 'He needs tender loving care – and bandages.'

Between them, the two girls and Matt the telegrapher lifted and carried Marvin across the room.

'Maybe now's the time to get my Greener from under the bed,' Madame Larkin mused.

Men were now tumbling out of the Tanglefoot Saloon and Talbot Hotel. Antonio was shocked to see so many. Why? Somehow, the kids had miscalculated the numbers.

It didn't matter, he decided. His job was to pin them down.

That's what he'd do. He fired with extreme precision – wounding the men in an arm or a leg, but careful not to fire a fatal shot.

From time to time, he monitored the corner of the street to his right – somebody was still there, they'd shot out the street lamp. . . .

While he maintained his blistering and accurate fire, he fretted about Naomi. Was she all right?

The outside walls of the Tanglefoot Saloon drummed, as if being pounded by hailstones. Heath Kendall sat at a table at the rear of the bar area, nursing a beer, wondering where he'd gone wrong. Maybe by blindly following his lieutenant. . . ?

'Hey, Kendall, why ain't you shooting?' Bernie demanded, swaying slightly as he approached the table. 'Are you turning soft on us?'

'You've had too much to drink, Bernie,' Kendall said, dismissively.

'Vince tells me you've gone soft on the sheriff's widow. Is that true?'

'Don't get me riled, Bernie.'

'I've had enough of you telling me what to do, dadblast you!' Bernie swore and whipped out his revolver.

Kendall fired his weapon from under the table, two shots that slammed into Bernie's thighs.

Bernie wailed, fell backwards, his pistol firing at the ceiling. Pieces of plaster dropped to the floor.

A couple of other men stopped shooting out the windows, glanced at Bernie writhing on the boards.

'I'm going up to the roof,' Kendall said, standing. He kicked the gun out of Bernie's hand. 'I'll see if there's some way we can stop that damned sniper!'

He holstered his gun, strode to the stairs and climbed them, studying the reflections in the bar mirror till he reached the half-landing and was out of sight. He let out a breath and continued up the two further flights to the roof exit.

Hitherto unarmed, Mateo carried Bret's gun and ducked inside the town hall doorway while Ramón was round the back, dealing with the explosives' fuses.

He had no cover and cursed as Hart shot at him, the bullet slamming into the door frame on his right.

His heart sank as he realized that Hart was using Banker Ream as a shield.

Hart levelled his gun at Ream's head. 'Throw down your gun, circus man!'

Josefa decided to leave the unconscious Pat where he lay. He wouldn't cause any trouble for a while, at least. And he wasn't going to bleed to death. She wiped the blade clean on Pat's shirt, tucked the knife in her belt behind her back and then retrieved the keys and unlocked the other cell. 'Come on, grab some weapons and follow me!'

Deputy Leavy selected a Winchester and holstered a six-gun. 'Just a minute, miss, where are you going?'

'The mine – they've freed the hostages there.'

'They have?' a man said, slipping a pistol into his waistband.

'How'd you know?' the deputy asked.

'My friends sent up a rocket, the signal they'd taken over the mine.' She bit her lip, was anxious to move. 'Come on, we need—'

'No, wait a minute,' the deputy said. He eyed the stack of weapons. 'I need to get these to some of the townspeople. You can go help your friends at the mine – my duty's to the town. I need to swear in more deputies pretty darn quick!'

Judge Park cleared his throat, nodded. 'Makes sense, Miss

Mendoza.' He reached for a rifle, ratcheted a bullet home. 'I'll go with you, Deputy. It's about time I fought for the law, instead of just wielding my gavel and passing down sentences!'

Josefa eyed the two men who'd shared the cell with Deputy Leavy. Neither one seemed like a fighter. One of them said, 'We'd like to go with you, Miss – it seems a mite safer.'

She couldn't blame them. East Street was a mere alley on this side of Main Street, cutting between the sheriff's office and the doctor's. Opposite the sheriff's office, however, it widened, cutting between the Talbot Hotel and Tanglefoot Saloon. They would have to cross the expanse of Main Street to get to the east end of town where the majority of the populace lived – and doubtless hid. 'Vale! Let's go, then,' she said and selected a Winchester with a full load.

Deputy Leavy and the judge stuffed a number of weapons into a sack then opened the front door. Leavy nodded at Josefa and the judge then sidled out. There was gunfire from the Tanglefoot and the Talbot – and they'd have to run directly between them to enter that side of East Street.

Foolhardy, Josefa thought.

Despite her misgivings, she pointed to the two men. 'Grab a rifle – we'll give them covering fire!'

The two men obeyed unflinchingly, taking a rifle each from the central pile.

She remembered Mateo's injunction. 'Aim for their legs – try not to kill any!'

One remonstrated, 'But—'

'They may be killers, but we aren't – unless we're forced to it,' she explained sombrely.

They rushed to the windows on either side of the door, smashed the glass with the snouts of their rifles.

'Go!' Josefa shouted.

Deputy Leavy and Judge Park hefted the sack between them

and stepped out. Josefa started firing her rifle at the group of Hart's men. Two men tumbled to the boardwalk, blood staining their legs.

'Go!' she repeated.

The men of law jumped to the hardpan and raced across the street.

She hoped that Antonio could see well enough to recognize the judge. To her left and right, her two men complemented her tirade of lead, their shots not particularly accurate, but they served their purpose.

Dragging four wounded, Hart's men backed inside the saloon and the hotel.

Josefa aimed to keep the men's guns and heads away from those windows that afforded a view of Leavy and Park, running at a slight angle to the saloon.

Once they'd reached that side of East Street, sheltered by the two buildings, Josefa shouted, 'Stop firing. They've made it!'

'Thank God,' said one of the men.

Then, from the smashed windows of the two buildings a withering response of lead battered the walls of the sheriff's office and shattered what little glass remained.

'Let's go before they think about rushing us,' she said.

Ducking low, they crossed glass that crunched underfoot. She led the two men out the back door. Clutching her rifle, she prayed to the Holy Mother that the shadows in the alley would be deep enough to conceal them.

They clung to the walls; and at the end of the alley, all three turned right and headed for the mine compound's entrance, unopposed.

His mind filled with the vision of the top of Chad's head shot off, Trampas shakily descended the bordello steps, looking left and right. He flinched as he noted that rifle fire came from the loft of the livery.

'Hey, over here, quickly, man!'

Across the street, in the shadows, a man beckoned. He didn't recognize the voice, but he sounded more like a friend than a foe.

He didn't fancy offering himself up for target practice to the livery shooter, so he dashed across the junction, his nerves on edge as he covered the distance, and then he breathed a sigh of relief as he dived into the shadows.

'What in tarnation's going on?' Trampas asked, breathless. That girl Charlene had sure taken it out of him.

'Hell if I know. Seems someone hid a rifle and is taking pot shots at your men, pinning them down.' He gestured across the street at the two bundles on the boardwalk. 'He got Chip and the undertaker a few minutes ago.'

'You're not with Hart, are you?'

'Nope – but I owe him for springing me out of jail. Name's Monty Blake.'

Trampas nodded. 'Yeah, I've heard of you.' He pulled out his six-gun, spun the cylinder, loaded the empty chamber. 'What are you gonna do?'

'We need to get round the back of the livery. Stop him treating your pals like fish in a barrel.' Blake coughed and spat.

Mateo lowered the six-gun and smiled, glancing out the side window. He perceived the shadowy shapes crossing the road and heading towards the mine compound. That had to be Josefa and the others from the jail. 'Well Mr Hart, despite all the shooting, we haven't killed any of your men.'

'We? How many of you are there?'

'My troupe. The Magnificent Mendozas.'

'Ah, I've heard of you!'

121

'I'm sorry I can't say the same about you, Mr Hart.'

'How do you know my name?'

'I have my sources.' Mateo sighed. 'Are you going to wave that gun under the banker's nose forever, or can we behave in a civilized fashion?'

'I say,' wheezed Ream, 'that's a good idea, sir!'

'I'm still doubtful about your magnificent people not killing any of my men.'

'I gave explicit instructions on the point.'

'Oh, really? What about Bret?'

'He's unconscious on the town hall steps.'

Hart shrugged. 'You realize you can't possibly win? I've got hostages in here and placed all around the town.'

'You *had* – we've just freed those in the mine *and* the jail.'

Hart stared, disbelieving. 'You can't have – that's not possible!'

'But it is, Señor Hart. We too now have hostages – and that includes your woman in the mine office.'

'My . . . woman. . . ?' Hart's face paled. 'You'd let them kill Emily?' He grated his teeth and moved his six-gun from his hostage to point it at Mateo. 'For that alone, I should shoot you where you stand!'

Seeing the splash of firework in the dark sky, José mounted the leader with a single lithe leap, second nature to a trick rider. He looked down at Gene, who seemed dwarfed by the shotgun he carried. 'Stay here where you'll be safe.'

His face quite serious, Gene said, 'I will, that. But where are you going, Mr Mendoza?'

'I'm going to the mine. Maybe I can be of assistance.' He wheeled the horse round. 'Take care, little one!' Then he was off, riding under the moonlight. He glanced to his right – there was the vague glow of false dawn on the horizon.

The plan was for him to free the hostages in The Passion

Flower, while Josefa was to take the hostages from the jail to the mine. But first he wanted to make sure she was all right. Her husband Mateo shouldn't have put her in harm's way!

He rode back to the town. A little guiltily, he glanced over his shoulder as he skirted the southwest edge, eyeing the smithy, tannery, church, livery and bordello. He led the horse behind the part-depleted forest and boot hill.

Within a few minutes, he was riding up to the gates just as Josefa and the others arrived on foot.

'What are you doing here, *amigo*?' Josefa said. 'You should be freeing the hostages at the bordello!'

'I wanted to make sure you were—'

'You should not be here, José!'

He shrugged. 'No matter, I'm here now.'

The gates opened and he had no time to exchange even a greeting as Juan let them all in and shut the gates after them.

José dismounted and joined the others as they clambered up the wooden staircase and crowded into the office.

When José stepped in behind Juan, his first instinct was to rush over to Josefa, but then he stopped and stared at Emily Chase. Although he recovered quickly, Josefa seemed to notice and asked, 'Do you know her?'

'No, of course not,' he lied. 'I was just surprised to see one of these desperados was a woman.'

'Why be surprised? The boys mentioned it.'

He shrugged and strode out again on to the balcony and studied the view of the darkened town, Mine Street and the town hall. He'd seen Emily's eyes narrow as he entered – his old flame had recognized him as well, but wasn't about to reveal that fact. . . . Her flaxen hair was in disarray, and her shirt had been torn. He glimpsed the cleft between her breasts and all the old passion he'd felt for her returned in force. His pulse raced, those heady memories rekindled.

*

Banker Ream broke the deadlock, abruptly elbowing Hart in the gut and shoving the man's gun hand down, buying vital seconds. Mateo's reactions were swift and agile; he leaped at Hart and grabbed the hand holding the six-gun, shoved it aside. Between them, Mateo and Ream grappled Hart to the floor and overcame him.

But there were two other guards here and now one of them barked, 'Leave the boss alone, or I'll shoot you down!' The pair levelled their rifles on Mateo and Ream.

Mateo glanced around – most of the hostages were women. In fact, the only male hostage was the mayor and he hadn't made a move to assist. He couldn't blame the man, not against two rifles. Reluctantly, Mateo raised his arms and the banker did the same. This was not good.

Groggily, Hart got to his feet, glanced over his shoulder at his men. 'What kept you?'

'Sorry, Boss, we were at the other end of the—'

Suddenly, Hart swung round and punched Mateo in the mouth. 'Tell me, now, where are your people?'

The blow numbed Mateo's jaw and cheek. Wiping his cut lip with a sleeve, he said, 'Most of them are in the mine compound, like I told you – it's quite a fortress.'

Hart shook his head. 'You're fools, all of you! We'll kill a hostage every half hour unless they surrender.'

'My people have instructions to kill the Chase woman first, then the rest of your men – one death for one death.'

'You're bluffing.' Hart shook his head. 'You're circus performers, not killers.'

Mateo smiled thinly. 'Before we joined this circus, we had to fight off Apaches and *federales* and bandits. We've spilled blood, I assure you, and have no qualms about spilling more –

especially that of outlaws.'

Hart peered out the window and nodded. He turned back to Mateo, his tone full of approval. 'I should have put someone in the livery loft – it's a good place. You'd have made a good soldier; I'd have been proud to have you on my side.'

'I don't take sides.'

'Oh?' Hart sneered. 'So what are you doing now, if not taking sides?'

'I'm fighting for what is right.'

'So I'm on the side of what is wrong, is that it?'

'You said it, Hart.'

'Well, I like to think I'm on the winning side. So, how many men have you in the loft?'

'Enough to keep your people pinned down.'

Hart shook his head. 'There are too many of us to beat.'

'More than we estimated, I agree. But the cavalry is on its way to even up the numbers.'

Hart looked out the window at the telegraph office. 'No gunfire coming from there,' he mused, 'so Theo must be out of action.' He turned to face Mateo. 'The cavalry troop will take a day, maybe two days' hard riding.' He smiled, pleased with himself. 'You can't manage a siege all that time. We have enough men to outflank your shooter.'

Mateo's heart sank; Hart spoke the truth.

CHAPTER 10

BOLAS

The mine office was stifling; José wanted to get out but he couldn't. Not yet. Standing in the doorway, he sucked on his quirly and scanned the room. On his left lay an unconscious desperado named Coburn and beside him sat another called Jesse, his eyes downcast at his boots, his back against the wall under the window. Leaning against the shelves of files was Emily, her eyes darting, as if she were scheming. Both she and Jesse were bound by rope around their wrists held in front of them.

It wasn't surprising the place was uncomfortable, considering that, besides their prisoners, on his right were Josefa, idly gazing out the window, the rifle in the crook of her arm, Mr Gray, the mine owner, at his desk and his daughter Naomi, seated in the only other chair. Fortunately, to ease overcrowding, the two townswomen, the four male hostages and the two men Josefa freed from jail had elected to go with the miners, Jamie and Donnelly, who had gone down to re-join their fellow workers, readying themselves for what might come at dawn. Janet McTavish had been overjoyed to fall into the embrace of her husband, Sheldon. Arcadia was outside on the balcony with Juan; José envied them the fresh night air.

By his reckoning, Juan would be his relief in about an hour. He walked over to the desk and dipped the mug into the water bucket and drank. It helped a little.

'Can I have a drink – some water?' Emily asked, her voice a croak. She nodded her head at the water bucket.

José scooped a mugful.

'Don't humour her, Señor Mendoza!' snapped Naomi.

He carried it to Emily, 'It's only water, *señorita*.'

'That bitch doesn't deserve any consideration.'

'Hush, now, dear,' whispered her father. 'Be charitable.'

Father and daughter began a whispered argument while José tipped the mug to Emily's lips. Between gulps, she said, loudly, 'Thank you.' And, in a low voice, she added for his ears only, 'You know they'll hang me for this.'

His heart tumbled. He screwed up his eyes, unable to visualize that beautiful neck stretched on the end of a rope. 'Why? You're a robber, not a killer.'

'If we lose this fight, you can bet there'll be a few dead townspeople. I don't see them waiting for a circuit judge – they'll lynch those of us who are left.' She looked at the floor. 'You'd better put a bullet in me now, José. . . .'

He gasped involuntarily and his hand trembled as he lifted the mug again. 'What if I helped you get away – if you promise not to harm anyone?'

She nodded. 'Yes.' She smiled, flicked her tongue over wet full lips. 'We could meet at Mesita. I'd wait for you.'

Her eyes became slightly hooded and his memory filled with the rapture of their time together. He'd lusted after Josefa but imagined that she was not as fiery as Emily. Until he met Emily, his experience taught him that Mexican women were the best in bed. Until Emily. . . . 'But what about Hart? I've heard you're his girl.'

She smiled seductively. 'I ran away from the Cantina and Hart saved me from the desert.' She shrugged. 'I've paid him for that.' She licked her lips again and they glistened, inviting. 'He means nothing to me.'

'You promise?'

'Yes, José, I promise.'

He glanced over his shoulder at the others. 'I'll have to wait for the right moment.'

'Don't wait too long,' she said, her soft breath on his cheek. 'I ache to be free – and with you, my José.'

That did it. With his back to the Grays, he unsheathed his knife, cut the rope around her wrists. 'Make it look good,' he whispered.

'I will – thanks. . . .'

'Quiet, Father,' Naomi said, 'I think – something's happ—'

Emily stepped around José and pulled his six-gun from its holster. She aimed it at Josefa and then Naomi. 'Don't make a sound, or it'll be your last!' she whispered harshly.

Naomi paled. Her father got to his feet, his face white, eyes fearful.

'You promised. . . !' José said softly.

'It won't come to that,' Emily said out the corner of her mouth. Then, loudly, clearly for the benefit of the others, 'Call your two circus pals inside.' She pressed the gun to his neck. 'Do it.'

Josefa raised her rifle.

Emily eyed Josefa, shook her head, and pressed the muzzle hard into José's neck.

Josefa relaxed, lowered the rifle to the floor.

'Arcadia, Juan!' José shouted. 'I have a problem!'

The door opened and Arcadia stepped in; she wasn't carrying her bow and quiver of arrows. Juan took in the scene at once and was about to lift his Navy Colt and back away out of sight when Emily snapped, 'If you both don't come in, your pal José dies!'

Reluctantly, Juan and Arcadia entered the office.

'Close the damned door!' Emily snapped.

Juan kicked the door shut.

Emily eyed Arcadia. 'Use your knife, cut Jesse loose. And don't try taking him hostage. He's useful but I can live without him.'

'Thanks for that,' Jesse said grudgingly.

When Jesse was free, he relieved Juan of his gun-belt and Colt, then picked up Josefa's rifle. 'And I'll take the knife,' he said.

Throwing daggers with her eyes, Arcadia handed it over.

'And yours,' Emily said, pointing her gun at Josefa.

Reluctantly, Josefa reached behind her, pulled out her Bowie and flung it point first into the floorboards at Jesse's feet.

With a little effort, Jesse pulled the knife free, and then gestured at the supine Coburn. 'What about him?'

'We leave him,' Emily snapped.

'I guess he ain't useful.'

'That's right, Jesse. Now, are you going to be happy about taking orders from a girl, or not?'

'All of a sudden I like it fine.'

'Good.' Emily gestured at Mr Gray. 'You – throw me your keys!'

'There's nothing of value in the safe,' he said.

'I don't want your safe – just give me your keys!'

He shrugged, opened the desk drawer and withdrew a small bunch of keys. He hesitated then threw them to her.

She caught them adroitly. 'Right, all of you back off – over there.' She indicated the corner to the right. As Mr Gray,

Naomi, Josefa, Arcadia, José and Juan moved, Emily added, 'No, not you, Miss!'

Naomi started, glanced at Arcadia and Josefa.

'Yes, little rich girl, you!' Emily gestured impatiently with the revolver. 'Come here!'

'Please, don't hurt my daughter!' wailed Mr Gray.

Naomi clung to Josefa's arm. 'I won't, I won't,' Naomi stated firmly, though her voice betrayed a tremble.

'If you don't do as I say, you'll be an orphan inside one minute.'

'All – all right!' Naomi hurried over to Emily, her face conveying a mixture of emotions.

'Good. You're coming with me until we're away safe – then I'll let you go.'

'Oh, God, no,' Mr Gray cried out. 'Take me, not her!'

Emily shoved Naomi towards Jesse. 'Take her out, keep her quiet. We don't want the miners alerted. I'll be along shortly.'

Jesse grasped Naomi and grunted. Docile now, Naomi went with him.

Backing to the doorway, her eyes never leaving them, Emily said, 'I'll give you all a chance to live.' She eyed José pointedly. 'I keep my word.' Then she reached behind her, grasped the hanging lantern by the door and flung it to the floor. It shattered, the oil spilt and the flame instantly spread across the boards, blocking access to the door. She darted out, slammed the door shut and soon found the key to lock it.

They couldn't get to the door; the flames prevented an approach from any direction.

Josefa glared at José. 'How'd you let this happen?'

'*Lo siento* . . .' José shrugged. 'I – I'm sorry.'

'We haven't time for this!' snapped Arcadia.

Juan grabbed the bucket of water and flung it on the flames

– but what little there was had no discernible effect; indeed, the flames spread.

'Water on oil,' Gray said, shaking his head. He ran over to the unconscious Coburn, grasped his wrists and, huffing and puffing, dragged him across the room, away from that side of the office. All five of them now stood behind the desk.

Juan smacked his forehead and swore. 'I might have used the water to bring him round.'

Arcadia rushed to the windows on the left; Josefa checked the window to the right: they overlooked the palisade but offered no safe foothold for a descent. The window behind the desk revealed a drop of some thirty feet to the entrance gate roadway. A last resort, but there was the certain risk of a broken leg or worse for some of them.

As they stood at the front door of the town hall, the eyes of all the hostages were on them. 'You, Greg,' Hart said, pointing to one of his two men, 'come with me.' He gestured at the other. 'You know what to do, Vince?'

The man's eyes narrowed. He turned, looked at the hostages standing by the meeting hall door – the mayor, his wife and six other women, and nodded. 'Sure, Boss.'

Hart opened the door, peered out. The shooter in the loft was busy pinning down his men at the hotel and saloon on the east side of the street. Why hadn't somebody gone out the back door and taken care of him yet? Damned imbeciles! He eased out, using Mateo as a shield. Greg followed, using Banker Ream for protection. Then came Vince, who quickly locked the door.

'That should hold 'em till it blows,' Vince said and skipped down the steps and ran round the corner towards the rear of the building, where Bret had set the fuses.

Hart glanced left and right and prodded his pistol into

Mateo's back.

'I thought you said Bret was on the steps, unconscious.'

Mateo shrugged. 'Maybe he got up, went for a walk.'

Hart slugged him with the butt of his revolver. 'Don't play games with me, you stinking Mex—'

Someone came round the corner.

'That was quick, Vin—'

But it wasn't Vince. 'Your pal Vince won't be lighting any fuses,' said the stranger whose left arm hung limp at his side.

'Ramón!' Mateo exclaimed, pleased but fearful.

Ramón's free hand swung his bolas around his head then let fly and they encircled the legs of Ream and Greg; the pair of them toppled down the steps. In the same instant, Mateo elbowed backwards at Hart, but received a glancing blow from the barrel of Hart's gun.

'Ramón!' Mateo shouted in alarm.

Too late. Ramón raised his knife to throw, but Hart's two quick-fire bullets slammed into the escapologist's chest and he sank sideways, tumbling to the ground.

Levelling his gun on both Ream and Mateo, Hart snapped, 'Come on, Greg, get up, damn you. We have a bank to rob!'

Luckily for them, the bank was just across the road.

'What about the silver?' Greg asked, disentangling himself from the bolas.

'It's a lost cause, thanks to these interfering Mexes!' He grabbed Mateo by the scruff of his neck, shoved him down the steps. 'Come on!'

The four of them ran awkwardly across the open space, towards the bank entrance.

From the shadows of the veranda, a Winchester ratcheted.

'Don't shoot, it's me, Hart!'

'What's happening, Boss? I've been here since I relieved Mack at supper time. Sounds like a war's going on!'

'You've done a great job, Tom. Join us. We're leaving town – after we pay the bank a visit.'

Outside on the balcony, Jesse said, 'Why didn't you just shoot them?'

Naomi gasped.

Emily sneered. 'Hush, girl, if you know what's good for you! I may be just a girl, Jesse, but I know that any shots would have brought a horde of miners down on us.'

'Yeah, of course, I should've thought of that.'

'Then,' Naomi said with a moan, 'you were bluffing?'

'Don't get me wrong, honey. If I need to, I won't hesitate to shoot – anybody.' She glanced down at the compound, which was lit by several torches in sconces on the building's walls. She smiled. 'We're in luck!'

'How?' Jesse asked.

She indicated the wagonload of silver bullion, standing next to the winch engine.

The windows of the miners' block were lit by a buttery light, but there was no sign of anyone coming out to see what was happening.

On their left were the stables. 'Let's get the wagon hitched,' she said.

'We could try smothering the flames,' said Gray and hurriedly outlined his idea.

Juan nodded. 'It's a good plan, I think.'

'Well, then, quickly, help me!' Gray started pulling out the drawers of his desk, piling them against the wall beside the safe. 'Now, move the desk forward and tip it over when I say!'

Juan, José and Gray pushed the heavy desk towards the flames.

'When we tip it, back away quickly!' Gray warned.

133

As they got closer, the heat from the door area became quite intense.

'Right,' Gray ordered, 'tip it *now*!'

The desk was big, broad and heavy, even without its drawers and their contents. It thudded on to its side and then they heaved again, forcing the flat expanse of the desk top to tilt towards the burning area at the base of the door.

The three of them hastily backed away as the desk fell and thudded on to the floor; draughts of air and flame spurted out from all sides, but it seemed that most of the flames were smothered.

'Quick now,' barked Gray, 'turn it round, as I said!'

The three men grabbed a corner and swung the upturned desk round so a far corner pointed at the door, while Josefa and Arcadia went to retrieve Coburn and then slumped him at their feet by the desk.

'Ready – heave!' Gray shouted.

All three men pushed the desk forward, and without much resistance the far corner splintered the wood of the door. Perhaps it was already weakened, since it appeared scorched.

'Again!' Gray urged.

This time, the door gave way, pieces falling, scattering, sparks flying. Small flames licked the sides of the desk, jumped hungrily at the varnished wood.

Josefa and Arcadia clambered over the base of the desk, ignoring the flames on both sides. Between them, José and Juan carried the unconscious Coburn outside to the balcony, then, casting a final glance at his office, Gray followed.

Breathless, Judge Park whispered hoarsely, 'I need to stop!' They were almost at the end of the block abutting this section of East Street. 'I'm not used to this kind of exertion.' He leaned against the wall of the Talbot Hotel and used a handkerchief to wipe his face and neck.

'OK, but just for a minute.' Deputy Dan Leavy lowered the sack to the ground. 'I'll go see what's happening.' He moved cautiously to the end and peered round the corner, first left then right. Then he returned to the sack.

'There's one of them pinned down at the south end of North Street – must be the shooter in the livery loft. Whoever he is, he's giving all of them a lot of grief.' He put a hand on the judge's shoulder. 'Do you reckon you can make it? We need to cross North Street and head for the row of houses.'

Judge Park coughed into his hand, glanced around; nobody came running. 'Surely, Deputy. Let's get this done.' He leaned down and lifted his end of the sack while Leavy grabbed the other.

They stopped for a moment at the entrance, but there was no chance that whoever was at the southern end of the street would see them. They rushed across the open space, into the last third of East Street. On their right was the fruit and vegetable store and a disused lot; on their right, serried ranks of houses.

'Follow me, Judge.'

Leavy gently tapped on the window of the first house. Luckily, the shooting didn't drown the sound and the occupant peered out at him. Widow McKenzie smiled when she saw him, signed for him to go to the front door.

Seconds later, she ushered them inside, shut the door, then led them into the parlour. Leavy and the judge lowered the sack to the floor.

'What's happening, Dan? How'd you get out of jail?' She glanced at the judge, her brow wrinkling.

'This here's Judge Park – he was jailed with me.' Maybe some other time he'd laugh at this, sharing a cell with a judge; but not today. 'Some of the circus people came back and let us out – they're putting up a good fight against Hart and his men, but I think they could do with some help.' He opened the sack. 'I've brought some weapons.'

'That's wonderful, Dan, wonderful. And thanks for helping us, Judge. Usually, this is a peaceful little town.'

'I'm sure it is, ma'am – and it will be again, if we prevail.'

'I thought we could round up a few people and hand out these guns,' Dan Leavy told her.

'Yes, of course. You stay here. I'll go out and send them in.'

'No, ma'am,' the judge said, 'that's a mite too risky.'

'You've taken enough risks already to get this far. Leave the weapons here and I'll bring you some people who know how to use them.'

'Lily's the general store owner,' Dan explained to the judge. 'She knows who's good with a gun, all right.'

Judge Park nodded. 'Very well. But take care, ma'am.'

'I sure will,' she said and left through the back door.

Within a short while, seven men and a woman entered through the back door with Lily. 'This should even up the numbers, I reckon,' Lily said.

Mrs Dent approached Dan. 'I'm worried about Larry.'

'When'd you last see him?'

'When I took him his supper – he's staying at the livery.'

'Well, he'll still be there.'

'Maybe . . . but there's a lot of lead flying.'

'He can look after himself, Rosanna.'

She nodded then stooped to pick up a shotgun from the open sack on the floor.

'You can't go, Rosanna – you're—'

'And why not?' interjected Lily, hefting a Winchester.

Judge Park smiled. 'I think you have enough deputies now, lawman.'

'Yeah, it looks that way.'

CHAPTER 11

JUDGE, JURY, AND EXECUTIONER

Coughing on the smoke, Josefa turned on José, grabbing his shirt. 'You let her go! What were you doing in there?'

'*Lo siento, mi chica. . . .*'

'Sorry? That's all you can say? And don't "*mi chica*" me, you swine! You almost got us killed!'

'I regret she outfoxed me – she is obviously a wily woman, but—' He looked away from Josefa's accusing, penetrating stare, and met the condemnatory gaze of Arcadia. He stopped, his mouth agape. '*Madre de Dios*, she's taking the silver!'

Already, Jesse had opened the gates and Emily was driving the wagonload of bullion through. Naomi was draped semi-conscious on top of the tarpaulin, blood streaming from her brow.

'Oh, dear God, Naomi!' wailed Mr Gray, grasping the bannister rail.

'No, she will not get away with this!' José leaped down the stairs. She'd betrayed him! He ran over to the stables and

137

quickly sprang on to the back of the nearest wagon horse. No time for saddle or reins. He grasped the animal's mane and urged the mount on after the wagon.

Turning to Mr Gray, Arcadia said, 'Watch Coburn; if he wakes, make sure he doesn't escape!' She grabbed her bow and quiver of arrows from the rail and then she and Juan raced down the stairs.

As she ran by Juan's side, heading for the stables, she noticed that Josefa was running to meet the miners coming out of their dormitories, led by Donnelly. She felt sure they'd deal with any of Hart's men who crossed their path.

Backed up by seven men, two women and the judge, Deputy Dan Leavy walked down the centre of North Street, his heart in his mouth, which probably explained why it felt dry.

Dawn streaked the sky to his left, creating long shadows.

Blake stepped out – clearly far enough down the street to avoid being hit by the sniper in the livery loft. 'Quite a welcoming committee you've got at your back, Deputy.'

'I'm taking you in, Blake. The judge is just behind me.'

'Seems like you've got a jury and an executioner there as well.'

'You'll get a fair trial, Mr Blake!' shouted the judge.

Blake shook his head. 'Nope. It might be fair. But I don't particularly care for a necktie party, even if it's legal.'

Leavy and his group stopped opposite the rear of the Tanglefoot Saloon. The shooting on the other side of the block seemed sporadic now. Maybe the sniper was running low on ammo, Leavy thought. 'I'd recommend you come quietly, Blake,' he called.

'Like hell I will!' Blake raised his gun and there was a volley of shots. Bullets peppered his torso. He sank to his knees and then fell head-first into the dust.

*

The fresh air was welcome after the stink of smoke, cordite and black powder. From here, Kendall looked down on Main Street and had a view to his left of the rooftops of the general store, butcher and shoe-smith, all single-storey buildings below. Then, beyond, loomed the livery, the loft opening about level with this roof. Behind him, the sun was rising, and aided visibility, but Kendall couldn't actually see the sniper, only the muzzle flashes. The sniper seemed to be conserving his ammunition, only firing if a target presented itself. Kendall wondered what kind of men Hart had recruited for this job. Not one of them had considered coming up here. A handful of riflemen could probably dislodge the sniper with ease. He checked to the right – and paused, surprised.

Crossing the street junction that faced the town hall was Hart and Greg, one of Calhoun's men. They were shoving the banker and a Mexican towards the bank.

Kendall swore. Hart was going to rob the bank and get away in the confusion.

'Well, Boss, you're going to be disappointed, if I have anything to do with it!'

Ignoring the intermittent shots from the livery loft, Kendall clambered over the parapet on to the roof of the Talbot Hotel. The next two buildings in the block were a storey lower, but he felt confident he could get down from there without attracting attention.

Greg and Tom stood inside by the bank's front door, their weapons trained on the banker and Mateo.

'Just open your safe, Mr Ream, and fill these,' Hart ordered, holding up two canvas bags, 'and then we'll be on our way!'

Grafton Ream folded his arms, his normally pale complex-

139

ion now flushed. 'I already told you, the townspeople have entrusted me with their money. I will not betray that trust, for you or anyone else!'

'Very noble of you.' Hart sneered. He turned to Mateo, levelled his revolver under his nose. 'You're a brave man, Banker Ream. Let's see how brave you are with this Mexican's life.' Hart thumbed back the hammer.

Mateo didn't blink or speak.

Hart grinned. 'Maybe you can catch the bullet between your teeth, eh?'

Mateo simply stared, unmoved.

Brow sprouting sweat, Ream wheezed, 'All right, I'll open the safe, damn your eyes! This brave Mexican came here to save us – I won't be responsible for his death.'

'Yeah.' Hart chuckled. 'I put you in quite a quandary, didn't I?'

'I think you're getting a bit too cavalier about people's lives, Boss.'

Pivoting round, Hart said, 'Kendall, how'd you get here?'

'Over the rooftops. It seems I was just in time to collect my share.'

'Yes, of course, I was going to share it with those of our men who get away.'

Kendall shook his head. 'You're a liar, Boss. You were going to run out on all of us!'

'You're the liar, Kendall!' Hart snapped. 'Every goddamned day you've put objections in my way. I'm getting sick of it!'

'There was a time when you respected women, and the lives of innocents.' Kendall sighed, adjusted his stance. 'It seems that time's passed.' He shook his head. 'I'm sorry, Boss, but you're not robbing this town of its hard-earned money!'

There was a blur of movement. Tom raised his rifle, aiming at Kendall. Hart drew his revolver. Kendall cleared leather.

Three shots sounded.

As the smoke cleared, Greg growled, 'Don't think about making a move!'

Both Mateo and Ream stood stock still.

On the floor lay the corpse of Tom, a bullet hole in his forehead. Kendall sat against the nearest wall, bright red blood oozing from his chest.

'You're a mite faster than you used to be, Boss,' Kendall said, coughing blood.

'And you've turned soft, old friend.' Hart knelt down, relieved Kendall of his weapon. 'Sorry about that.' He straightened. 'But I have a bank to rob.' He turned to Banker Ream. 'All right, let's open your safe!'

Antonio was distracted by the shooting around the corner of North Street. He was also concerned that he was down to his last three bullets. And he fretted over Naomi – where was she, and was she all right?

Pat regained consciousness in the sheriff's office. He was surprised not only to be alive, but also to find he was unfettered. His head ached, his wounded arm was sore as hell and his stomach heaved. Suddenly, he disgorged the meal that woman had brought. He recalled his earlier hasty visit to the privy. Maybe she had poisoned it? Nah, he was sick probably due to the blow that Mex bitch had given to his head.

He got to his feet and swayed unsteadily. Casting about, he noticed there were still a few guns lying in the centre of the room. So they'd taken most, but not all. Too many to carry, likely.

Shooting was sporadic, and seemed to be coming from the south end of town.

He walked to the guns and picked a Colt, winced as the wound in his arm made its presence felt. Gritting his teeth against the pain, he checked it was loaded and shoved it in his holster. He glanced at the back door, which was open.

If he could get out the back, rush down West Street and go to the livery, he thought, he could get a horse. He sure as hell didn't want to stay now. Too much shooting. Silver or no silver.

He rushed to the back door, and then slumped against the doorjamb, his head swimming, giddy. Whoa, take it slow and steady, he told himself, his head ringing, as if he was recovering from a bender.

Standing beside the judge, Deputy Leavy turned to the others. 'Thanks for your help. We're going to go in the back of the hotel and saloon now, clear out any who are left there. I'm asking for volunteers, but I'd rather not take women.'

Lily said, 'This is my town, Dan. I'll fight for it, just like you men.'

'I'm going to find out what's happened to Larry,' said Rosanna Dent, reloading her shotgun.

'Do you want one of us . . . ?'

'No, Dan, you clean out those hoodlums. I'll be just fine.' She strode purposefully towards the southern end of the street.

Two men held back, but the rest of Leavy's posse stepped into the back doorways of the Tanglefoot and the Talbot.

Guns blazed.

Loaded with silver bullion, most of it covered by the tarpaulin, the wagon careered down Mine Street, Emily cracking her whip above the heads of the two horses. On top of the tarp sat Naomi, holding her bloody head and firmly gripped by Jesse.

In seconds, they approached the town hall. 'Look, it's the boss!' exclaimed Jesse, pointing to the corner of the bank building.

Hart and three others were just stepping out of the bank.

Hart had two weighty canvas bags slung over his shoulders. His revolver was held against a Mexican's head, while Greg covered the bank manager with a rifle.

'Whoa!' She hauled on the reins and applied the brake. 'Come on,' she ordered, 'I've got the silver!'

'And I've got the money,' Hart replied, keeping his gun on Mateo.

'Pleased to hear it,' she snapped. 'Now, let's go!'

With his free hand, Hart hefted the moneybags into the rear of the wagon. He eyed Naomi, still held firmly by Jesse, and grinned. He turned, thrust Mateo away from him.

Mateo bumped into Banker Ream.

Greg shoved the banker aside, laughing, and ratcheted his Winchester.

'We only need one hostage, circus man,' Hart said, 'and she's a mite prettier than you!' And he fired.

In the same instant, Ream thrust himself in front of Mateo, screaming, 'No!' The bullet penetrated the banker's back and he collapsed against Mateo.

Greg raised his rifle but he wasn't quick enough.

In the blink of an eye, Mateo unsheathed the knife from his boot and threw it. The blade sank into Greg's right arm and he staggered against the veranda post.

Emily screamed, 'We haven't got time for this! Come on, Roger!'

Hart swore, jumped on the wagon and fired over his shoulder at Mateo as they pulled away.

Greg fired in Mateo's direction, too, while running along the boardwalk after the wagon. He jumped and landed awkwardly on the tarp-covered silver bullion. Naomi shrank away from him.

Emily drove the wagon down the side of the bank. She looked over her shoulder.

José was following on a horse and some way behind him, came two more riders.

She turned into North Street.

The thoroughfare was deserted. She was surprised to see a corpse lying in the middle of the road, but skirted it and urged the horses on.

Not for the first time, Alice stood on a soapbox at a window of The Passion Flower, watching the pretty ladies in the salon. One day, she'd like to wear one of those colourful dresses. This time, though, she was distracted as she saw movement at the end of Hallahan Road. Her blood ran cold. It was the man named Pat, the one who killed Emmett's pa. He was sneaking across the road, moving towards the livery.

Emmett was there, still. Mr Rivera was up in the loft, but he hadn't seen him.

Fearful for Emmett, she got down from the box and raced across the end of the street. Must warn him. . . .

As Emily swung the wagon team round the corner into Hallahan Road, she spotted a young girl in front of her, in harm's way. She couldn't – wouldn't – stop.

CHAPTER 12

DEATH IN THE LIVERY

In the same instant, a blur passed Emily and the wagon's horses.

With great acrobatic skill, José clutched the mane, leaned down from his horse, snatched Alice, lifted her up and thrust her in front of him.

It was too good an opportunity to miss. Holding the reins in one hand, Emily drew her pistol and fired at José's back.

José slumped forward. Alice held on to the mane as their mount slowed.

Suddenly, Emily's wagon was past them and she turned again, passing the livery and tannery on one side, the church and smithy on the other, heading for the Mesita Road.

The wagon careered round the corner of the shoe-smith, into Hallahan Road, directly under the livery loft. Antonio gasped at the plight of young Alice in its path. He was helpless, there was nothing he could do; he was out of ammunition.

He almost cheered when José scooped up Alice from almost certain death. Then his heart lurched as he saw José shot in the back and, in the same instant, he noticed Naomi, semi-conscious in the rear of the wagon.

He rose, discarded the rifle, and slid down the loft ladder. 'Mr Dent, I'm borrowing a horse, all right?'

'Sure, you do what's necessary, son.' Dent tucked a thumb in his coveralls and hefted his shotgun. 'I'll hold the fort here.'

'*Gracias*!' Antonio mounted a buckskin and rode out the rear of the livery, following after the wagon.

Emmett ran to Dent's side, said, 'Where's he going?'

'Never you mind, son. Go on, get inside and hide till all this dadblamed shooting is done.' Dent clasped a hand over Emmett's shoulder and they walked back inside the livery. 'I've got chores to do – they don't stop needing to be done just because there's a little gun-battle going on, you know!'

Trampas had hidden against the wall of the feed and grain store, next to the livery. He couldn't understand why Monty had stepped out in front of that mob of townsfolk. He'd stayed in the shadows at the end of the street, feeling quite alone and fearful. Then he'd checked the two corpses, found money on both and pocketed the bills. That sure would help.

Now, as he counted the money, he'd just seen the silver wagon go past. He swore. The swines were leaving with the loot!

He must grab a horse. He thought of pursuing the wagon, but reckoned he'd be no match for three men – and that Emily Chase was a mean bitch, too. No, Hart could keep his silver. He just wanted out. . . .

He snuck round the back of the livery. His luck was in. A couple of chestnut mares were pacing round the corral, probably disturbed by all the shooting. That makes three of us, he thought, and rushed to the corral and slipped between the poles. He walked up to the nearest horse, whispering soothing words, gently extending his arm. The horse tentatively approached him, lowered its head and he stroked it. 'You and me are going to get away from all this noise, eh?'

He glanced over to the back door of the livery. Just inside were several saddles, reins, bits and bridles. He ducked under the pole, rushed over and helped himself.

'Where in tarnation do you think you're going?' demanded Larry Dent, raising his greener.

Trampas lowered the saddle to the ground. 'Hey, go easy, mister, I was just borrowing—'

'I don't think so,' said Dent. 'You're one of them desperados, hell-bent on bleeding our town dry!'

'No, I ain't. I've got money, I'll pay!' With slow considered movements, he fished in his vest pocket, pulled out a wad of dollar bills. 'See?' He proffered them in his left hand.

Dent's eyes widened into saucers. 'Why didn't you say so in the first place?'

'I didn't – didn't shout because I – I didn't want to – to draw the attention of my – those desperados.'

Nodding, Dent said, 'Makes sense, I suppose.' He lowered the shotgun and held out his hand for payment.

'How much for the horse, saddle, the lot?'

'What you've got there should cover it, son.'

'OK,' said Trampas, 'since you asked for it.'

As Dent's hand closed on the money, Trampas swiftly drew his revolver and slammed the barrel against Dent's temple.

Dent fell to the ground, the bills scattered, and he groaned, his eyes seeming unfocused.

Trampas holstered his gun and scrambled after the notes, collected them all, and shoved the bundle into his vest pocket. Then he drew his gun again, aimed it at Dent. 'I'm sorry, old man. One more shot ain't going to be heard above the racket that's going on in the town. *Hasta la vista*!'

He cocked the revolver.

'Sorry.'

Abruptly, his body jerked as shotgun pellets spattered his torso, back and front. He briefly danced, jerkily, like the marionette of a deranged puppeteer, and collapsed on his back. He shuddered and shook, his lips quivering, his gun juddering in his grasp.

Pat slunk through the small gap between the partially opened livery front doors. It was dark, many sections of the place darker than outside; about three yards away was a coal oil lamp, casting its welcome light. He blinked at the lamp's contrasting intensity, heard the shuffling of several horses. He noticed the back doors were wide open. That was the best way to ride out, once he'd stolen a mount. Get the hell out.

'St – stop there, put your hands up, don't m-move!'

The voice was shaky, definitely young. Until he could gauge who was threatening him, he decided to comply and raised his hands. 'Who's there? I'm just a lonely traveller.'

Pat heard the distinctive noise of a six-gun's hammer being cocked.

'What – why? St-step slowly into the light, mister, and no tricks.'

'All right.' Pat moved forward slowly, one step at a time. He looked left and right, trying to determine where his armed questioner stood.

As he entered the lamplight, he distinctly heard a gasp. What the hell?

'You – you're the one named Pat.'

'Yeah, so? What of it?'

In answer, his interrogator stepped into the light too. It was just a boy! But, he allowed, the boy carried a six-gun, which was cocked. Sure, the gun seemed too big and heavy for the lad to handle, but that made no never mind if it went off in his face.

'Hey, boy, should you be playing with guns? They're kinda lethal, you know?'

'Oh, yes, I – I know that for sure, mister. My pa was the sheriff, so I know all about guns.'

Sheriff? Christ, he was the sheriff's kid! Yes, now I recognize the little squirt. 'Hey, you were there, you know it was a fair gunfight. I just won, that's all.' He thought he'd better throw in a bit of sympathy. It worked, sometimes. 'Sorry it was your pa.' Saying sorry didn't hurt, neither. Hell, he didn't mean it; it was a lawman, for God's sake!

'You can surrender now and go to jail for my pa's murder.'

Pat noticed there was no hesitancy, no stammer in that statement. He's a game shaver, I'll give him that. He glanced to the stalls, where a few horses seemed nervous. Nervous? Hell, they should try being on the end of a cocked gun held by a kid!

'OK,' Pat said, deciding to play along till he could get the drop on the little bastard. 'I'll surrender.'

'Throw down your gun where I can see it.'

This was it. 'Sure, kid.' Pat went for his revolver, drew it fast; it was a blur.

Abruptly, his vision blurred in more or less the same instant. A bright flash blinded him and the gunshot deafened him and an almighty pain hammered in his chest. He felt his legs lose all power to support him and he thudded on to his knees.

Hazily, Pat noticed the kid stepped forward a pace, the revolver cocked again, the barrel still emitting a thin sliver of smoke.

Tears glistened in the boy's eyes.

'That's for my pa,' the boy said, 'and this is for my ma.' He fired again and the light of Pat's world went out.

'Sorry. . . .' echoed in his head, but it wasn't his voice, even though he recalled saying that word. Trampas blinked, the massive pain in his body almost robbing him of any cohesive thought.

Vaguely, he recognized Madame Larkin standing over him. At her shoulder was another woman; he reckoned it was the one from the restaurant he'd visited when off duty. 'Sorry,' this woman now repeated, 'but I couldn't let you murder my husband in cold blood.'

Shakily, he beckoned to Madame Larkin. His lips moved, barely, his voice a strange, hoarse whisper, 'Tell . . . tell Charlene she was the best thing to happen to me in my life.' He fumbled in his vest pocket, pulled out a wad of dollar bills. 'Here, give this to her – she was worth every damned cent.'

Trampas coughed and died.

Antonio rode in pursuit of the wagon. He heard the pounding of horses' hoofs behind and glanced over his shoulder. He breathed easy, as it wasn't any gang members, but Mateo; it looked like he'd mounted poor José's abandoned horse. And behind him were Arcadia and Juan. He smiled. That evened up the odds.

The odds were evened further when Arcadia fired an arrow. This one had a sharp point; it pierced Greg's eye and he tumbled off the wagon.

Naomi screamed as Jesse fired and his shot hit Antonio's right hand.

Antonio reined in briefly, let Arcadia overtake him. Mateo rode alongside him and quickly wrapped a bandanna round the wounded hand, then, seconds later, they were giving chase again.

*

As the wagon passed a large boulder, young Gene scrambled to the top of it, shouted and then fired his shotgun. He was thrust backwards with the recoil.

The shot peppered the side of Jesse's face and shoulder and he lurched against Emily. She was hit in her cheek and arm and dropped the reins. Jesse fell off the wagon, rolled in the dust and lay still.

Alarmed by the close proximity of the shotgun blast, one of the horses veered and stumbled, lost its footing and broke a leg.

Abruptly careering on two wheels, dragged by a single horse, the other wounded animal shrieking in pain while still in the traces, the wagon lurched and shuddered over the ground.

Then the traces snapped, the remaining horse ran free and a wheel slammed against a massive rock and shattered. The wagon crashed to the ground, shuddered along, spouting dust clouds and dirt, and then slid over the lip of the narrow Parnham Gorge.

CHAPTER 13

CLIFFHANGER

Antonio's heart tumbled. He drew his horse to a halt, jumped to the ground and ran to the churned earth at the lip of the gorge.

His mouth went dry, but at least his heart began to pound again.

The wagon had fallen some ten feet and was now wedged between two boulders protruding from the side of the gorge. The front half of the vehicle and the tongue hovered and rocked, suspended in the air.

Naomi and Emily must have been thrown forward with the sudden movement and now clung to the tongue, their legs dangling. The drop for them was at least fifty feet, the bottom of the gorge jagged rocks.

About ten feet below the wagon, Hart clambered down the side of the gorge. He was abandoning the two women. Slung over his shoulders were two bulging sacks.

Silver bullion was scattered among the rocks below, though the majority was still in the wagon bed, but some of that began to slide slowly towards the seat, unbalancing the precariously swaying vehicle.

Arcadia and Juan halted their mounts, jumped down and rushed to Antonio's side.

'Save Naomi!' Antonio barked. He lay full length on the ground and leaned over the lip of the gorge, extending his left arm.

Mateo rode alongside them. 'Hart's getting away!' he said, gazing over the lip.

'Juan and I can do this,' Arcadia said. 'You get him, Mateo!'

Juan scrambled over the edge. 'Grab my ankle,' he ordered Antonio and flung himself down.

Antonio snatched Juan's ankle and let out an involuntary grunt as he took the trapeze artist's weight. The pair of them dangled over the edge; Juan's out-flung hand was about five feet away from Naomi.

The wagon lurched as Emily moved, trying to clamber back on board. The right arm and that side of her face were covered in blood.

'Please, help me!' Naomi cried.

Arcadia dived head first over the edge, and Juan deftly snagged her ankles.

Antonio groaned at the sudden jerk and the added weight.

It was enough. Arcadia's hands wrapped around Naomi's outstretched wrist. 'Got you!'

In the same instant, Emily scrambled up the tongue and leaped, missing Naomi's leg but grabbing hold of the hem of her skirt.

Antonio let out a yell. 'Oh, *Dios*! My arm, I can't hold you all!'

Mateo climbed down, nimble-footed, moving faster than Hart because he wasn't encumbered by two bags full of stolen money.

Hart paused, raised his Smith & Wesson and fired. The shot zinged off a rock to Mateo's left, quite harmless. 'You damned Mexicans! They had the right idea in Ranchería!'

Hart's words pained Mateo. His uncle had been one of the innocent Mexicans the citizens of Ranchería had slain in '55. But that was mob violence, not the true will of the people.

He shrugged off the blanket of cold hate and slid down a section of scree, coming to a halt in a cloud of dust by a boulder.

Another shot, closer this time, ricocheted off the boulder.

Still, he was about ten feet away, and gaining.

Sensing the tugging weight of Emily on her skirt hem, Naomi loosened her belt, let the skirt ride over her hips and slide off her.

Emily shrieked, frantically clasping the garment as she fell; her shoulder hit a big rock some twenty feet down, the bone-crunch almost drowning her scream. She held on, but only briefly, as the wagon lurched again. Silver bullion tumbled out, and a couple of bars thudded into Emily's face. Abruptly, she relinquished her grasp on the rock and fell to the bottom of the gorge, where she lay twisted, broken and still.

'I'm going to swing you towards the side of the gorge,' Juan shouted to Naomi. 'Hold on, Antonio!'

'I'm trying, I'm trying!' His voice was strained.

Slowly, painfully slowly, Juan began swinging Arcadia back and forth, with Naomi dangling at the end of their human chain.

'When you're close to the rocks,' Arcadia called, 'let go and jump!'

Naomi cried, 'No, I can't, I can't!'

'You've got to, Naomi. Antonio can't hold us much longer!'

The rock face rushed toward her, receded, came again.

'Next time, Naomi!' Arcadia called.

'My arm!' Antonio shouted.

'Oh, Antonio!' Naomi wailed and let go, thrust herself forward. For a brief instant she closed her eyes and thudded into the rock face, among a jumble of small boulders and stone. Her heart leaped, she felt solid ground, stone, and opened her eyes. Her hands like claws, she clung on for her dear life. 'I made it!' she called, jubilant.

In seconds, Juan let go of Arcadia; she somersaulted, twisted in the air and her hands clasped Juan's, just as if they'd been performing on the trapeze in the big top. Then she scrambled up Juan's body, and leaped up past Antonio. Juan was beside her in a moment.

Hart watched Emily fall but didn't hesitate in his scramble down the side of the gorge. He was about halfway down now. He anchored himself against an outcrop, swung round and fired up at the damned Mexican.

Mateo ducked one last time and threw a knife. The blade sliced into one of Hart's moneybags. The coins spilled out.

Hart shouted in surprise and twisted round, grabbed for the coins and notes as they scattered. But in his panic he lost his foothold and stumbled from rock to rock, gaining momentum as he fell, the boulders splashed red to mark his abrupt final descent.

EPILOGUE

THE MAGNIFICENT
MENDOZAS

Boot hill was crowded – with the living. It was intended to be a sombre occasion yet, despite the recent deaths, a strong sense of liberation couldn't be dampened. The entire population of the town assembled around the graves, and to the fore were Emmett and Gene with their parents and a tearful Alice. Lily McKenzie stood beside Heath Kendall, supporting him; he wore a sling and his chest was heavily bandaged.

In the past, there might have been discrimination, but not today: the Mexicans José and Ramón were interred next to Banker Ream, Undertaker Perry and Sheriff Rosco.

Reverend Christie praised brave men who put the community before self, and thanked God for deliverance in the guise of the Magnificent Mendozas.

Among the remnants of the Mendoza troupe stood Naomi Gray. 'Your hand, Antonio,' she whispered, tentatively touching his arm held in a sling.

He turned his gaze from his friends' graves. 'It will heal, but

I'm probably finished as a sharpshooter.'

'I'm forever in your debt, Señor Rivera,' said Mr Gray, gently clamping a hand on Antonio's shoulder.

Antonio winced – that arm had almost been pulled out of its socket in the early hours of that morning. '*Mi placer*,' he said.

'If you wish to leave the circus,' Mr Gray added, 'I have need of a good man at the mine.'

'Thank you, sir.' Antonio glanced across at the others.

Mateo stared down, doubtless still blaming himself for the two deaths in his troupe. Earlier, Antonio had spoken to him. Mateo said that if he hadn't listened to the two boys, his younger brother would still be alive today. Antonio countered, 'José was an adult, he made his own choices, and that involved women, too, my friend. By our actions, we probably saved many lives in this town.' Mateo had nodded, not entirely convinced.

Arcadia and Josefa let their tears fall, but held their heads high. Juan stood quite stoic, perhaps because the dead were not his relatives, only his companions. On either side of them, the miners led by Donnelly offered their sympathy and support.

Donnelly had fought alongside Josefa as they cleaned up the last vestiges of desperados. By seven in the morning, the town had been re-taken and over the following hours it had gradually returned to a semblance of normality.

They'd used the mine compound to cage the surviving desperados who had surrendered. Then, under armed guard, these same prisoners were coerced into digging a mass grave at the far end of boot hill.

A simple plaque was commissioned and would name those known with the warning inscription: *Here lie evil men who were consigned to hell by the Magnificent Mendozas and the townspeople of Conejos Blancos.*

Mining was suspended and the prisoners would be kept in the compound until the cavalry arrived.

*

Diego Vallejo smiled as the Mendoza wagon approached. Mateo drove, with Josefa by his side. On horseback were Arcadia and Juan. As the wagon drew up in front of him, his smile froze when he saw their faces.

'Where are the others, *mis amigos?*' he wheezed.

'We lost José and Ramón,' Josefa said, her eyes glistening.

He let out a groan. 'And Antonio?'

Mateo said, 'He has left the troupe – his wound prevents him from performing.'

Diego sighed and his lower lip trembled. 'I told you, warned you. . . .' He brushed a hand over his goatee. There was despair in his voice. 'You are finished as an act, no?'

Arcadia rode up, her voice strong, defiant. 'No, Diego. We are not finished. We are strengthened. Seven of us freed a town from over thirty desperados!'

'But at what cost?' Diego demanded.

'The fight against evil will always cost noble lives,' Mateo said. 'It is in the nature of things. But good will prevail.'

Josefa nodded. 'Be assured, Diego, the Magnificent Mendozas *will* perform again.'